Whose dark or troubled mind will you step into next? Detective or assassin, victim or accomplice? How can you tell reality from delusion when you're spinning in the whirl of a thriller, or trapped in the grip of an unsolvable mystery? When you can't trust your senses, or anyone you meet; that's when you know you're in the hands of the undisputed masters of crime fiction.

Writers of the greatest thrillers and mysteries on earth, who inspired those that followed. Their books are found on shelves all across their home countries—from Asia to Europe, and everywhere in between. Timeless tales that have been devoured, adored and handed down through the decades. Iconic books that have inspired films, and demand to be read and read again. And now we've introduced Pushkin Vertigo Originals—the greatest contemporary crime writing from across the globe, by some of today's best authors.

So step inside a dizzying world of criminal masterminds with **Pushkin Vertigo**. The only trouble you might have is leaving them behind.

THE MASTER KEY

PUSHKIN VERTIGO

TRANSLATED BY SIMON GROVE

MASAKO TOGAWA

Pushkin Press
71–75 Shelton Street
London, WC2H 9JQ

Original text © 1962 by Masako Togawa

Translated by Simon Grove

Every effort has been made to contact the owner of the rights to this
translation. Please contact Pushkin Press if you are the copyright holder.

The Master Key was first published in Japanese by Kodansha in 1962
First English translation publish by Dodd Mead, 1985
First published by Pushkin Press in 2017

1 3 5 7 9 8 6 4 2

ISBN 13: 978 1 782273639

Designed and typeset by Tetragon, London
Printed and bound by CPI Group (UK) Ltd, Croydon CRO 4YY

www.pushkinpress.com

THE MASTER KEY

PROLOGUE

1 April 1951: At the Otsuka Nakacho crossroads

On that day, the snow (unusual for April) which had fallen on the night before was still half an inch deep in the morning.

But before midday the sun peeped through the clouds and a thaw set in. In no time at all, the streets once again danced in the sunshine of spring.

At exactly noon, a woman tried to cross the road at the Otsuka Nakacho crossroads, even though the lights were against her.

Her head was completely hooded by a red scarf, and she wore a thick winter coat over black ski pants. This in spite of the fact that everyone else on the street was beginning to sweat slightly in the warm sunshine...

When the woman had got about a third of the way across the road, a small van came racing towards her from the direction of the Gokokuji temple. It was fully laden with wooden kegs of nails. The young driver, a boy from the mountains, was affected by the snow; his mind was full of the rosy-cheeked girls of his native place, and he had his foot hard down on the accelerator as he came up the slope. The green light seemed to beckon his youthfulness on—hurry! hurry! it seemed to say. From the corner of his eye, he caught a sudden glimpse of the girl in the red scarf but to him it was just a further reminder of the girls in his snow-bound native village. Perhaps that was why he skidded on the tramlines, although one cannot be sure. At any rate, the inexperienced young driver slammed on his brakes, but the van did not respond to his efforts to control it. It slid right around and headed back towards the woman. The last thing the young man saw before closing his eyes was the red-scarved and astonished face of the woman as she came crashing through his windscreen.

It took three minutes for the white ambulance to come from the fire station a hundred yards from the junction; it sped away with the casualties, and in another three minutes had delivered them to a nearby branch of the T University hospital. During this time, the girl opened her mouth and muttered something three times, but no one could catch what she was trying to say. By the time the ambulance reached the hospital, it was over.

A tall, white-coated doctor examined the body and pronounced it dead.

'In spite of the lipstick, this was a male,' he added in a strangled voice. His face was quite expressionless.

Those present had difficulty in repressing their laughter, until they were overcome by the solemnity of death, so that even the horror of the traffic accident was driven from their minds.

The young driver, who had been but the instrument of destiny, was punished beyond reason. He was in deep shock, and even after admission to the hospital he seemed unable to close his mouth. He slavered constantly, and kept muttering disjointedly, but all he could say was, 'The red scarf, the red scarf.'

Time passed.

The busy police detectives waited for a family to come forward and identify the body of an unknown male, aged about thirty, who wore female dress...

Time passed.

A cub reporter covering crime, with time on his hands, went around the homosexual world of Ueno showing the photograph of the unidentified male...

Time passed.

The doctors and nurses at the hospital gradually ceased to joke during tea-breaks about the unidentified male, in female dress, who had been run over at the Otsuka Nakacho crossroads.

But somewhere, a woman waited alone in a darkened room... waited for the man to come back to her.

The room was on the fifth floor of an apartment block, buried in the shadows just two bus stops away from the Otsuka Nakacho crossroads.

She awaited the return of the man whom she had dressed in her own red scarf, winter coat and black ski pants, the man who had gone off with slumped shoulders, without even looking back.

She waited, alone, for seven years. She is still waiting.

The name of the building where she lives is 'The K Apartments for Ladies'.

PART ONE

Three hints

The eye-witness: Three days before the accident

The man stumbled yet again as he climbed the stairs. The Gladstone bag that he was carrying seemed to get heavier and heavier; already, he had had to stop on the landing of the third floor to change hands. He gazed at the brown dyed leather bag, cursing its weight, but betraying no emotion towards its contents. He was too far gone to think of that any more. All he was now concerned about was getting everything over with as soon as possible. He had been driven along for the last few hours by a feeling of resignation, a hope that the end was at last in sight. His consciousness seemed blocked by a wall, or blinded in limitless darkness. Now that the end was at last near, he felt no elation, merely a sense of despair.

Shrugging his shoulders, he wiped his forehead with a handkerchief and carefully readjusted the red scarf around his face before picking up the leather bag again. The sweet female perfume on the scarf affected him profoundly. Recovering his spirits, he lifted the heavy case and carried it, bumping his knees, up the staircase. From time to time, he could hear footsteps or voices downstairs. Hurrying on, he reached the fifth floor and, pausing only to make sure there was no sign of life in the corridor, made his way to the door of a certain apartment.

A girl was waiting there. Glancing at the travelling bag, she asked, 'Did the receptionist say anything?'

'No, she was so deep in her newspaper that she didn't even notice me.'

As he replied, he lowered the case onto the doorstep. The leather base curled and the bag overbalanced onto the concrete floor with a dull thump.

'Hey, watch what you're doing! You shouldn't treat it so roughly!' exclaimed the girl in a loud voice.

The man wanted to point out how heavy the bag was, and how his hands were slippery with sweat. But he could only mumble, 'It makes no difference.'

The woman, without seeking his help, lugged the bag into the middle of the room.

'Poor little thing. Well, we'd better get him out quickly.'

'Poor little thing.' The woman repeated herself, but the man could only slump on the floor and gaze blankly at her.

The woman snapped apart the clasp of the bag, which fell open. Inside, there was the body of a small child. She unwrapped the thick blanket, revealing miniature features in apparently tranquil sleep.

His silky flaxen hair glimmered like gold in the lamp-light. The girl chattered ecstatically.

'Oh my, oh my! Poor little fellow—we must get you out of this, mustn't we now? What a good little boy to put up with such cramps for so long!'

As she bent down to draw the little blanket-swaddled body from the bag, she noticed for the first time that he was gagged with a white handkerchief stained with clotted black blood. After a while she spoke, but her voice now had a hollow ring to it.

'He's dead.'

The man propped himself up on his elbows.

'It couldn't be helped. It was the only way.'

For a long while, all was silent in the room. The man and the woman just sat there with the corpse of the child in the travelling bag between them.

Ten hours later, the man once again took up the bag and set off downstairs. The woman led the way, flashing a torchlight down the stairs and along each corridor, making certain that no one was around. Taking their time so as to avoid making any noise, they finally reached the airless basement. There was a large tiled bath—about fifteen feet square—designed for communal bathing, which had not been used for some years. The man shone the torch around, picking out in the light various objects left scattered about when some construction project had been abandoned. There were a pick and shovel, a broken paper sack full of cement, a slime-encrusted wooden tub full of stagnant water, a heap of tiles… Last of all he shone the torch into the very centre of the bath, revealing a hole, about three feet deep, dug down beneath the tiles. He gazed at it intently; just as the woman had said, it was exactly the right size to take the Gladstone bag.

He handed the torch to the woman, and, tipping the contents of the cement bag out onto the floor, began to shovel it into a mound. Some of the cement had already set into hard lumps, but by dint of shovelling and flattening, he was at last able to form a little peak. Taking a little tin, he made several trips to the tap and, filling it each time, poured the water onto the cement. Every time he turned the tap on, the pipes rattled and wheezed alarmingly. But, nervewracking as this was for both of them, he persevered and at last the cement began to soften and crumble into a sludge. The woman opened the bag. The child was invisible under the blankets. She began to shovel the liquid cement into the bag; when it was full, she closed it and placing her hands on it spoke gently:

'What a beautiful coffin we have made!'

'Yes—it's quite conceivable that the body will never decay,' replied the man in a low voice. Although his face was running with sweat so that he could hardly keep his eyes open, he could waste no time before picking up the bag and hauling it to the centre of the bath. The woman drew a handkerchief from her bosom and mopped his brow. Then the two of them dragged the bag, which had become enormously heavy because of the cement, to the hole, which proved to be too narrow to accept it. Regardless of the noise, the man seized the pick and widened it where necessary. He knelt in the bath and crammed the bag in. It only remained to fill the hole with cement; the woman helped him; when it was full, they pressed the cement level with their bare hands, which turned red and raw as a result. Then they carefully laid tiles to hide the cement.

They were so engrossed by their labours that they failed to notice that a third person was hiding in the shadows and watching them.

The visitors' book

When the 'K Apartments for Ladies' were first opened, various strict regulations were ordained to govern the behaviour of the young residents. Nowadays, however, they had all reached mature years, and most of the rules had become a dead letter. But some had acquired the force of precedent and continued to be observed, the chief and most strictly observed of which was that it remained absolutely forbidden for members of the opposite sex to stay overnight in the apartments. Females could spend the night there provided they first reported to the reception desk.

But most of the occupants had become old maids, living isolated lives without friends or acquaintances, and so since the end of the war it had become rare for outsiders to visit or stay the night. All of which being so, there was still nothing so very suspicious about the entry in the visitors' book showing that Chikako Ueda, Room 502, had a close relative staying with her during the nights of 29 March to 1 April 1951.

The name of the guest was Miss Yasuyo Aoki.

Years later, when the police were looking into the matter of this female cousin, they questioned both of the receptionists. Their memories were by then hazy, but their testimonies agreed on one point—without question she was a woman.

One of the receptionists, Katsuko Tojo, having testified that she was on duty at the time that Chikako Ueda first brought her cousin to the apartment, went on as follows:

'I'm quite sure that Miss Ueda told me that her cousin would be staying with her for a fortnight. Yes, of course it was Miss Ueda who filled in the visitors' book, while her cousin just stood gazing out of the window. I don't particularly remember exchanging any conversation with her. Maybe it was her clothing, or perhaps they said she was from the Snow Country, but anyway she certainly had a rustic look… yes, that's it, she had a red muffler wrapped round her head. From the next day, Miss Ueda came to the office alone and filled in the visitors' book. Well, it's merely a formality—no need for the guest to come and do it herself. But after three days, she stopped coming. I never set eyes on the cousin again—she must have left about that time, I just can't remember, it must have been when Tamura was on duty.'

Katsuko Tojo went on to cover herself by adding that as she had a bad leg, and could only move with the aid of a stick, she was largely confined to her seat when on duty and so could not really tell what was going on.

Her partner, Kaneko Tamura, testified as follows:

'You ask me if I remember Miss Ueda's cousin carrying a large bag? Please excuse me—my memory's got so bad recently. I even forgot to pass on a telephone message yesterday, and the representative of the third floor is on to me about it! Well, if I can't even remember a telephone call, you can imagine how little confidence I have in my memory nowadays. So you can see why I can't remember about Miss Ueda's younger cousin seven years back. Oh—excuse me—I do remember something after all. She was strikingly pretty. Deliciously chubby, and very fair-skinned—but I'm not sure, really.'

The sum of the evidence given by the two women amounted to no more than the fact that, as the person in question was dressed like a woman and looked like one, it seemed unlikely that anyone would have taken her for a man.

The newspaper article

The story of the kidnapping of George, only son of Major and Mrs D. Kraft, aged four, did not break in the press until about the middle of April 1951.

The kidnapping took place on 27 March; the reason it was not made public until over a fortnight later was that the parents did not at first inform the police, but negotiated with the criminals secretly. They agreed to pay the ransom in two parts, the child to be returned on receipt of the second half. This was indeed an arrangement to the advantage of the kidnappers.

At least, that is what Major Kraft said, but as there were no witnesses, who could be sure of it? Because it appears that after arranging on the telephone for Major Kraft to deliver three hundred thousand yen to a certain spot (and he has never revealed where) the criminals broke off all further contact, although the Major persistently sought to re-contact them by advertising in the press. For several days, he inserted a three-line advertisement in every major daily paper:

'Keep your promise. I will keep mine. D. Kraft.'

This caught the attention of a certain journalist, who was thus able to scoop the kidnapping. But even after the fact became widely publicised, the Major resolutely refused to call in the Japanese police. Instead, he gave an interview to the press and his message appeared beside a photograph of him and his wife.

'All I want is to have the child back. I absolutely will not call in the police. I will carry out my promise completely— you do the same.'

They looked haggard. It seemed as if the Major was prepared to trust the kidnappers to the very last. Inevitably, the tragic sight of this gentlemanly foreign officer won people's sympathy. Moreover, it was plain from his attitude that he believed the criminals to be Japanese. This was clear from his reply to the persistent questioning of a journalist when he revealed that the telephone message was in broken English; also, his advertisements were written in Japanese, and he had not placed them in the English-language papers.

Another interesting point was that Mrs Kraft was a Japanese. Her maiden name was Keiko Kawauchi, then aged twenty-four, and she had met her husband while working in the Ginza PX. It was a typical example of a mixed marriage at the time.

But after a little, public interest evaporated like the melting snows of spring.

It never became clear why Major Kraft so obstinately refused to call in the police, or take more positive steps at the time of the kidnapping, but it is known that one year later he divorced Keiko Kawauchi and returned to the United States. It was also strange that the Military Occupation authorities were completely silent about the whole matter.

PART TWO

During the construction work

Miss Tojo Reflects

This morning, although I had sprinkled water over the office floor, everything on the desk was soon covered in dust and felt gritty—most unpleasant! We've been plagued by dust every day since the construction work started, but today, what with the high wind, it's been particularly difficult. When I open the heavy front door, the corridor acts as a funnel and the air is full of fine dust so that no amount of sprinkling will lay it.

But today should see the back of the task broken with the moving of the building. In thirty minutes' time, the whole building will be moved four metres, with all of us inhabitants in it! For the last three months, they've been digging out the foundations and laying rails under the structure. Now, a crowd of workmen have gone into the diggings and will work the fifty hydraulic jacks installed there so as to lift the whole building at once. The five-floor apartment house is shaped like a three-sided rectangle; excluding the basement, there is a total of one hundred and fifty rooms connected by dark corridors into which the sunshine never penetrates. There used to be an incinerator in the central courtyard, but it has been taken down to aid the work of moving the building.

The square behind is already crowded with a mob of rubberneckers. A television broadcasting van has just arrived and, pushing through the throng, taken up position in the centre of the square. It looks as if they're just about ready to start filming. In contrast, all within the apartment block is as quiet as the grave. Everyone is secluded in her room awaiting the moment the building will be moved.

It's my turn to be on duty, so my opposite number is also in her room. I don't feel at all comfortable sitting here all on my own. Comparing my watch with the clock on the wall behind me, I see that it is now twenty to twelve—that means I've got another twenty minutes to wait. I don't feel like reading a book or a paper to pass the time, which hangs heavy on my hands. Sitting here vacantly, I feel it quite natural to chat to myself. The phrase goes round and round in my head—'just a little while until the moment'—but precisely *what* moment? True, the office where I have sat for over thirty years, and this brick building of five storeys which has survived the great earthquake and the wartime air raids, has to be quietly moved, but is this what we residents are awaiting? This is surely just the outward appearance of the matter; being objective, which is to say looking at it from the outside, we won't actually be able to see the building being moved.

'We won't disturb you at all. You can all carry on living in the apartments just as before. You will see—you can fill a glass with water and we shan't even spill one drop when we move the building.'

Such were the words of the important-looking gentlemen who had come to persuade us to accept the plans for widening the road. They were a Section Chief of the City Highways Department and the Departmental Manager of some construction company. We had opposed the earlier

20

plans—tearing down half the building to make way for the road, or alternatively driving a tunnel through the lower three floors—and so they had come to win us over with the third plan. As a result of their explanation, given like a conjuror's patter in their most coaxing voices, we gave way and have since become inured to living amidst the construction work, and we're now cooped up like guinea pigs, literally holding our breath as we await the final event.

Man is an animal that seeks to know the reason for his existence, and just as a prisoner will scratch the wall of his cell to ascertain that he is still alive, and to mark the passing of time, so we guinea pigs had become so obsessed by the promise not to spill one drop of water that we agreed to put them to the test. It was Miss Shimoda, committee representative of the third floor, who first proposed this experiment. As she had originally been a science teacher, and was naturally devoted to experiments, it was perhaps a slightly strange outcome that she should have persuaded the majority to partake in what was after all a rather unscientific experiment. For the consensus was not for all to conduct a standard experiment, but for each to lock herself in her room and carry out the test in her own fashion. There was to my mind a certain irony in this. Still, as the practice of the ladies living in the apartments has always been to live their own lives without interfering in the affairs of others, it could not be helped. So that is the reason why all went to their rooms and locked themselves in an hour ago, providing the contrast between the bustle outside and the tomb-like stillness within. The only sign of life is Miss Iyoda's cat, which she has locked out of her room. It is curled up asleep on top of the banister on the gloomy staircase.

As for my views on this experiment—well, I think it's childish, not to say stupid. But, as a caretaker here, I have to be sensitive to the psychology of the residents—what looks like mere child's play in fact gives them something to be interested in. And as it is my duty to do what the majority of residents want, I too have put a glass full of water on the centre of the office desk.

Anyway, putting such thoughts aside, when I look at the water piled up to the brim of the glass, its surface like a living membrane, I remember first learning about surface tensions when I was a student, and how a speck of dust can break through it at any time; and I wonder if they are all so engrossed in this experiment just because they wonder if it will spill?

My answer is a definite No! The moment this building is moved, a past crime will be revealed. People are frightened that something will occur. That's why they avert their eyes, preferring to stare instead at glasses of water.

About six months ago, a clap-trap new religious cult called 'Oshizu' was very fashionable in this building. An unpleasant-looking man of about fifty, his hair plastered down with pomade, brought a girl no taller than a child known as 'the Thumbelina priestess'. I suppose they called her a priestess because she was dressed in a white robe with loose red trousers. Just like a shrine vestal, anyway, she danced some weird whirling jig. At first, only a few of the residents associated with her. But then, after a bit, she started making prophecies and miracles and the number of believers rose. There are still some who stick like I do to the first impression that she is a fraud, but the majority are now under her influence. When I say the majority, I mean most of those who spend the daytime in their rooms—in other words, the old women past retirement age. Those who still have work to keep them busy seem to be less involved.

But for some reason or other one thing haunted everyone's minds—the theft of the master key some two months before. This one key, meant for the use of the wardens, can open every one of the hundred and fifty rooms in the building, and is still missing. For the last six months, everyone in the building has more or less lived in dread and uneasiness. After all, the women who have lived alone for so long in these apartments have their secrets, little aspects of their lives known only to themselves, and now someone unknown is free to pry into them, to intrude.

As for myself, although I've spent nearly all my working life as a receptionist here, and haven't been able to get about much, not even to see a film or two since my leg went wrong, and although I must as a result appear a bit eccentric, it's not really so. I've enjoyed reading since I was a child, and try to understand the way of life of as many people as possible; I carefully read several newspapers every day, and hope I haven't fallen behind the times. But most of the residents here have at some time or other had the opportunity to lead as full lives as are open to women. Now, as they grow old and look back on the bright days of their pasts, a lot of them perversely withdraw into their shells. When I sit in my office by the front door after those with jobs have left, I shudder as I look at the silent staircase and think of those women in the building who will spend their remaining days in solitude, as if imprisoned by concrete walls. They merely stay alive; they have no activity except to dream about the past. At such times as this, I have a sort of hallucination: I imagine how, in rooms on the third floor, the fifth floor, old women pass their days in silence still gazing at the broken fragments of the dreams of youth, every now and then letting fall a sigh that echoes down the corridor, until they combine on the stairway and roll down to the cavernous hallway, raising one long moan around where I sit.

To such old maids, their little secrets are all they have to live for, all that gives them pride, all that remains of their possessions and estate. I think that the desire to pry into such secrets is reflected in the meaningless experiment with the water glasses.

From the small window of the reception office, I gaze out through the massive glass doors of the hall which shut me off from the world outside. I can see everything that is going on out there. I can see the mob outside, thronging the square and not the slightest bit put off by the choking dust that fills the air. They jostle one another as they try to peep into the foundations. Looking at them from my side of the glass, I wonder what on earth it is they are expecting. They are waiting just like a child waits who has wound the spring of his toy as far as he can, and holds it tight before letting it go. Or are they perhaps waiting to see the hole left behind when the building is moved? Perhaps they think it's like excavating an ancient tomb—perhaps they wonder what will be brought to light? 'This old red-brick building has stood here for fifty years, since it was designed by a young foreigner with the aim of helping Japanese women emancipate themselves; once aforetimes, passers-by would gaze at it with envious curiosity, this house reserved exclusively for single young ladies! Now the long years have wreaked an equal havoc on both the building and its inhabitants. What secrets, carefully hidden for so long, will now be revealed in the clear light of day when the building is moved? Beneath the ground lie immured what ghosts of yesteryear...?'

Are they lured by such trite images? Is that why they are waiting? That young housewife there, for instance, the one with a baby on her back and a shopping basket in her hand—what is it that has driven all thoughts of shopping for lunch out of her head to make her stand there with the rest? Is it after all just a short break in her busy life—just a few lost moments one noontime, I wonder? Or does she dream of witnessing—just one chance in a hundred—the collapse of our building?

Whilst I have been conducting this meaningless conversation with myself (a habit I've acquired naturally when sitting alone in the office; usually when I'm in a good mood it just happens spontaneously), time has passed and it's now five to twelve. A vigorous-looking young man has stuck his head out of the window of the television broadcasting van; he's waving his hands about. Oh, I see, the knock-kneed man in charge of the operation is going over to talk to him... he's wearing a safety helmet. They're having words—now the foreman is running towards the porch! He's opened the glass doors—making his way to my window. What can he want?

'Can I borrow the phone, please? The removal's been delayed thirty minutes—all because those television boys want to record the historic moment. Can you beat that? They went over my head to do it, too! Just because *they're* behind with their preparations, *we* have to wait. All they can think of is themselves—what about my workmen who've been standing by their jacks all this time?'

He's really upset! He's going to break the dial on the phone the way he's wrenching it! There goes the noon siren, and the jacks were supposed to be operated at exactly twelve. All the residents will be staring intently at their glasses of water! What tomfoolery! I don't know why, but this delay disturbs me too. The crowd outside are making disappointed gestures. Footsteps on the stairs—someone's coming down—it's Yoneko Kimura from the fourth floor. She's not going outside—she's going down to the basement. Funny look on her face! And here comes another. Michiyo Yamamura from the fifth floor. Her slippers slap the wooden floorboards as she makes her way over to me. She's in a panic, all right!

'The water spilled! I was just walking along the corridor on the fifth floor and Miss Ueda's door was open! I saw the glass on her table move! The water spilled! It spilled! And Miss Ueda too—on the table… she…'

But here's another interruption! Yoneko Kimura, back from her trip to the basement.

'Excuse me—it's vital. Could you please unlock the door to the old bathroom downstairs?'

And now the foreman's shouting at the top of his voice—trying to get something through to whoever's on the other end of the phone.

'What? Dig it up with pickaxes? Unnecessary, I tell you, just leave it to us. That bathroom's not concrete, you know.'

Let's see what's going on! Everything seems to have gone crazy since they postponed the removal. Out I go into the hall—now I'm losing my head too, I forgot my crutch!

PART THREE

Six months before the building was moved

Miss Tamura plays her part

Compared with Katsuko Tojo, who was older, the other desk clerk, Kaneko Tamara, was rather a gossip, but the residents of the K apartments found her amiable and easy to get on with. When on duty in the office, she would pass the time poring over newspapers or magazines, or else knitting with oversized needles, and seemed one of those worldly custodians who hardly ever glared at those coming and going in an ill-humoured manner. The truth of the matter was that she indulged in a secret pleasure whilst serving her turn of duty. She had perfected the art of catnapping at the desk in a manner not easily detectable from outside the reception window. For this old woman with no particular hobbies and without the pleasures and cares of daily family life to keep her occupied, catnapping at the desk was just a game to be played with other people. It also brought back to her some of the thrill of snatching forty winks during a strict teacher's lesson when she was a schoolgirl. Certainly, the effect of this daytime napping was a disrupted cycle and sleepless nights, but on the other hand she was also thereby able to avoid some of the boredom of office routine.

On that day, too, she had been sitting at the desk since three o'clock perusing a pamphlet called 'You and Your Palm', which someone had left on the desk. What with the heat from the charcoal stove at her feet and the pocket warmer in her bosom, she began to feel more and more sluggish as she tried to compare her line of destiny with those shown in the book, and dozed off again. At which point, someone came to the reception window. Kaneko Tamura went through her well-tried routine of pretending to have been wide awake, creaking her chair and turning the pages of the pamphlet with apparent interest.

But for once she could not drive from her head the passage she had been studying before dozing off—the page on the line of destiny. One of the many examples shown stayed in her mind—the broad line of destiny running straight to the base of the middle finger such as has been found on the hands of famous men. It floated before her eyes, preventing her from sleeping. She dozed only fitfully; the force and potency of the line of destiny loomed over her consciousness, giving her bad dreams.

Toyoko Munekata, a classmate of hers at secondary school, lived on the second floor of the apartment building. Now, she seemed to appear before Kaneko in her dream, berating her: *'How much longer are you going to carry on this sort of work? A lowly receptionist—a disgrace to our school, I tell you!'*

It was not as if she felt resentful towards Toyoko Munekata's status in any way, nor did she receive such treatment from her. But in her heart of hearts there lurked a feeling that she had fallen behind her in life, and this gave rise to a slight feeling of resentment. Since their schooldays together, there had existed between them an uneasy relationship, with Toyoko demonstrating the part scorn, part pity, that one has towards a stray dog. However, six years before, Toyoko Munekata had suddenly moved into the apartments and from then on had become increasingly immobile.

On that particular day, Miss Tamura had been sitting peacefully at the office window and, in her usual manner, was thinking about having a nap. Without any warning, Toyoko Munekata, whom she normally only met once or twice a year at school reunions, appeared from nowhere in front of her desk. Miss Munekata, watching the startled flush colour her face, took her time and, revelling in Miss Tamura's reaction, said:

'Well, well, what a surprise! How long have you been doing this, then? When we last met at the Old Girls' reunion, I distinctly remember you saying that you were growing roses in your daughter's nursery garden!'

At the time, she had felt thoroughly humiliated but gradually this weakened and was replaced by a feeling that it had been only natural for Toyoko Munekata to mock her so.

The dream changed, and now Toyoko was wearing thick-lensed glasses and the uniform of a high school girl. The scene was the examination hall, and all around her girls were busy scribbling answers with their pencils, but Kaneko was just sitting there, unable to write anything. Her paper was quite blank. However hard she tried, she couldn't understand the questions. There was nothing for it but to peep at her neighbour's paper. The girl beside her was suddenly transformed into Toyoko; she was covering her paper with both hands, purposely refusing to let Kaneko have a look. 'Please let me see,' she begged, but it was no use. Suddenly, all the other pupils vanished, leaving her alone with Toyoko.

She felt, as she dreamed, the deep disappointment and worry of that moment.

She cried out in despair, and at that moment awoke, dribbling. The pocket warmer which she had placed in her bosom had slipped over under her armpit. Wiping the sweat from her forehead with the back of her hand, she peered uneasily out of the window. Surely someone must have heard her cry out! Fortunately, not a soul was to be seen in the gloomy passageway, and all that could be heard was the distant sound of street musicians advertising a shop.

She leaned back in her chair and tried to drive the memories of the nightmare from her mind. She was helped in this by one of the residents coming through the front door; reaching down into the basket by her feet, she drew out the ball of wool and knitting needles and began to count the stitches. But she couldn't keep her mind on her knitting. She seemed to hear the echo of Toyoko's mocking voice lingering in a corner of the room, and could not overcome her depression.

Every now and then she put down her knitting and, resting her elbows on the desk, wondered why it had to be that a classmate whom she had hardly seen for so many years had fortuitously moved into this block of flats. She cursed the cruel irony of the situation, but did not know who to blame. Short of being angry with Toyoko, there was nothing she could do. And the annual class reunion was imminent. Since Toyoko had become a resident, Kaneko had not attended a single reunion. Every time, Toyoko had set off in her best clothes, never bothering to suggest that Kaneko accompany her. 'Can't I even do such a simple thing as attend a class reunion once a year… just a little white lie, that was all… It was a small enough pleasure for me, but…' Thinking these thoughts, she began to feel more and more resentful towards Toyoko. Just at that moment, the front door opened, and a young man in a suit came to her window.

'I'm from S University, and I was wondering if by any chance this is the residence of Professor Toyoko Munekata?'

Kaneko's head swam as she suddenly heard the name of the woman who had been occupying her thoughts. Nobody had come to call on Toyoko for at least six months. For a few seconds she just sat and gazed blankly at the visitor and then, remembering her role, stood up and offered to conduct him to Miss Munekata's room. And pulling open the drawer in her desk, she took out one of the numbered tallies which males had to wear when visiting the building.

'Excuse me, but could you put this round your neck? It's the rule for gentlemen who visit here, you see.'

The young man smiled graciously and, timidly extending his left hand to receive the tally, asked, 'How is Professor Munekata progressing with her important labours?'

Kaneko at first could not believe that this question was being addressed to her, and then was annoyed at having to honour Toyoko with the title of 'professor'. However, she at last recovered her wits sufficiently to chat to the young man.

'Professor Munekata always seems to be very busy. Whenever I pass her room, she seems to be busy with her studies—yes, and something else, she's really fussy about fresh air. The handle on her window doesn't work too well, so from time to time she complains to us about it. But however much we get it mended, it soon breaks again. Sometimes she leaves her door open, complaining of the lack of oxygen in her room. At such times, when I pass by, I notice she's always sitting at her desk. Everyone here remarks on how hard she works. Oh, and please don't forget to let me have the tally back when you leave; sometimes, guests forget and go out wearing their tallies.'

Meanwhile, she conducted him up the stairs. As she became more relaxed, she noticed that he was carrying a wrapped box of cakes, and realised that he was paying a formal call.

The door was ajar, and Toyoko could be seen sitting at her desk.

'Excuse me. You have a visitor.' She knocked, but there was no reply. Toyoko seemed to be engrossed in the paper before her on the desk. It was at least one minute before she turned towards the door and stood up.

'Who is it?'

'I'm from S University, but—'

'Come in, then.'

She beckoned the guest into the room and then, ignoring Kaneko, shut the door in her face. Kaneko bit back her humiliation and made her way downstairs, pausing every now and again to look at her palm. No, her line of destiny was too short, and also broken in two parts.

'Indeed, it has been long since I had the pleasure of meeting you. Today, I have come to call on you, Professor, and receive the manuscript.'

32

The young visitor stood before Toyoko, bowing politely and behaving with correctness. His hostess showed little concern; without bothering to offer him tea and cakes, she just pointed to a threadbare cushion on the floor. She then turned her back on him and stood by the large old-fashioned desk, left to her by her husband, which dominated the room. It was covered with manuscripts and ink-stained pens, bespeaking a busy existence.

There being no reply to his remark, the visitor sat uncomfortably on the worn cushion, and, looking up at Toyoko, who was sitting on a swivel chair at the desk, returned to the topic.

'We disciples of the late Professor realise how much toil you are giving to the correction of the manuscripts he left you. We feel that the time has now arrived for us to offer you what assistance we can.'

Toyoko swivelled the chair around so as to face him.

'I am the only person qualified to carry out this task.'

'Indeed, we quite understand that.'

'My husband's manuscripts contain ideograms that only I can read.'

Then, gazing at the ceiling, she continued in an offhand tone, 'From the day I married him, I spent my time rewriting his manuscripts. That was why we had no children.'

The visitor, moved by the pathos of this story of married devotion to an aged scholar, strengthened his resolve to obtain and publish the manuscript as soon as possible.

'We have completed all preparations for publication. We would very much like to have the manuscript—perhaps you could just give me those parts you have completed so far?'

The chair swivelled again, and Toyoko faced the desk, displaying to her guest the bent back of an old woman who has borne the burdens of others.

'As I've repeatedly told you on the phone, I cannot hand any part of it over until the whole is completed. You know that.'

After this outburst, she shut up like a clam. The visitor gazed on her unmoving back and reflected how the same excuses had been made, year after year, to all his predecessors. They had encountered the same stubborn refusal to compromise. He realised that today, also, he would have to return empty-handed; reaching into his pocket, he took out an envelope and placed it a little distance from Toyoko's feet.

'It is truly impolite of me, but if you can make use of this in any way…'

Toyoko displayed no reaction whatever. The visitor made no further reference to the manuscript and, after expressing a few formal sentiments, took his leave. At the top of the staircase he paused for a moment and gazed back towards the room. A thought crossed his mind— perhaps the reason for Toyoko's refusal to hand over the manuscript lay in its value; without having seen it, he could not say, but perhaps some commercial publisher had examined it and was negotiating for it at a high price. But could that really be so? It seemed unlikely that such a manuscript would fetch a large sum. Surely not; it was only as a tribute to the late Professor's war record that his pupils had collected a sum of money to ensure its publication. There was no question of its having a commercial value.

Comforted by these thoughts, the visitor set off down-stairs with a jaunty step, removing the tally from his neck as he went on his way.

Back in her room, Toyoko opened the box of cakes and, removing one, sliced it carefully with a small bamboo knife. As she ate, she ecstatically counted and recounted the money her visitor had left in the envelope. After a while, she returned to her desk and, assuming a busy countenance, took up an ancient German fountain pen which fitted exactly into a groove worn by writing in her index and middle fingers. She wrote the number '711' on a sheet of paper, and energetically proceeded to scrib-ble in a sort of shorthand of her own. At three pm on the same day, just after the changeover of duty at the reception office, the phone rang. Miss Tamura had just arrived, and Miss Tojo was still standing by the desk, with an expressionless face. Miss Tamura gazed at her and then took up the phone.

'Hello, this is the K apartments.'

A man was at the other end of the phone; he spoke in flat tones. Miss Tamura strained to hear his words, but found it difficult; screwing up her face in concentration, she gazed once again at Miss Tojo. She was about to say something when the line went dead. She shouted into the receiver.

'Hello! Hello! Don't ring off! Who is it?'

But to no avail. Gripping the receiver tightly, she stared vacantly at the desk until her colleague asked, 'Who was it?'

'Er… well…'

She struggled for words. Somehow, she didn't want to answer, but she had become so used to treating Miss Tojo as her superior, even though they were equals, that she found it difficult. At last she replied.

'Wrong number, I think.'

'Oh well, see you later, then.'

And Miss Tojo, not feeling like pressing her colleague for further information which she was plainly reluctant to give, thereupon left the office. The monotonous echo of her crutch echoed dully in the corridor for a while.

The office was dark and chilly. Miss Tamura stirred the embers in the charcoal brazier and busied herself for a few moments examining the duty register, then got up and went to the locker at the back. A notice stating the regulations governing the use of the master key was pasted on the locker door.

1. *The key may only be used in the presence of a witness.*
2. *It may only be used in an emergency.*
3. *The key must be returned to this office immediately after use.*

She stood in front of the locker for a while, subduing some inner conflict, and then shrugged her shoulders and went back to the desk. For a while, her customary faraway look was replaced by an earnest and penetrating stare as she pondered on the telephone call that she had just received. Who on earth was that fellow? What did he mean by suggesting that if she wanted to uncover a secret she should peep at the manuscript in Toyoko Munekata's room? It was all too nonsensical to bother about—just a practical joke, no doubt.

But when she had taken the student visitor to Toyoko's room, she had noticed a pile of manuscripts on the desk.

Was there really some secret buried in that enormous heap of papers? If so, then...

She tried once again to drive the thought from her mind, scrutinising the duty register which still lay open on top of her desk.

(Date.........)
Long-distance phone call (to Kiryu city)—Miss Takebe,
    2nd floor, 3 minutes.
Collection of gas bills
1st floor Complete
2nd floor Complete
4th floor Complete
5th floor Complete
Note Chase representative of 3rd floor about this.
Cat mess in 2nd floor corridor. Admonish owner.

The letters danced before her eyes, and seemed to lose all meaning. She picked up her abacus and tried to concentrate on totalling the pile of receipted gas bills, but to no avail; every time, the answer came out differently.

It was no use; the memory of that phone call lingered persistently in her mind, and she could think of nothing else. From that moment on, one thought dominated all others—how to get into Toyoko's room. Some day soon, when Toyoko was out, could she not use the master key? Surely no one would find out... Toyoko would certainly leave the building at some time when she was on duty. Kaneko thought of the locker and of the master key which she would inevitably be tempted to use. It was not as if she was moved by any criminal intent, but rather by the additional excitement brought by a moment of daring into the life of one usually given over to laziness and sleep.

Because of this, she soon brushed from her mind the fact, dangerous and startling as a snare suddenly discerned, that behind the telephone call lay a knowledge of her feelings towards Toyoko Munekata and the will of the caller to manipulate her to his own ends…

Miss Tamura climbed the stairs, one step at a time, ruminating on human nature. She paused fearfully on the second-floor landing, for she heard the sound of someone coming down from above, but mercifully the footsteps trailed off to another corridor on the upper floor. Heaving a sigh of relief, she tightened her fingers around the master key in her pocket.

She could not afford to be seen entering Toyoko's room, and prayed that none of the residents would be about. The excitement made her sweat.

Toyoko very rarely left the apartments, but today she had gone out early. Half an hour ago, she had phoned from long distance announcing in her usual aloof manner that she was heavily involved in discussions with her publishers. She would not be returning before ten pm and therefore her evening milk delivery was to be cancelled.

The message echoed in Miss Tamura's head with the insistence of an alarm bell. This was surely going to be the best chance to look in Toyoko's room for some considerable time. Feeling slightly guilty, Miss Tamura had approached her colleague Miss Tojo.

'That was from Miss Munekata. She doesn't want her milk this evening.'

'What? Does that mean she won't be back tonight?'

'No—she'll be back about ten. She's having discussions with her publishers.'

'Why, that means she must have nearly finished her manuscript. That's marvellous!'

'Yes. Oh, I nearly forgot. I've got a relative coming up to Tokyo tomorrow, and I'd rather like to take the day off. If it's all right with you, I'll swap with you—I'll do today, I mean.'

Miss Tojo consented readily. 'Of course. Well, I'll be off. It's a bit early for it, but I'll have a long bath. Cheerio, then!'

Miss Tamura blessed her luck. It was pure chance, plus her own quick thinking (and a lie) which had given her the whole day alone with access to the master key and her colleague safely away at the bath-house.

As soon as she saw Miss Tojo leaving with her washing things under her arm, she took the phone off the hook, collected the master key from the board, locked the office door and stealthily made her way upstairs to the second floor. She was almost in a trance, driven by a sense of some inevitable duty.

She tiptoed towards Toyoko's room, trying to prevent her rubber sandals from making any noise as she went. She stopped in front of the door, trembling as she stared at the name, written in beautiful calligraphy: 'Munekata'. Glancing around once more to make sure that no one was about, she hurriedly put the master key into the lock, but it did not seem to fit. She pushed and twisted with all her might, using both hands as if to force the lock. Suddenly the key turned with a loud grating sound and the door creaked open a few inches. She perceived a faint scent—the particular smell of the air in Toyoko's room—and her senses reeled, half from fear and half from curiosity.

She quickly closed the door and locked it from the inside. Pausing an instant in the tiny entrance lobby, she felt a twinge of guilt which she quickly dismissed before pulling aside the curtain and peeping into the apartment.

The room was very untidy. Against one wall there was a collection of worn furniture in faded colours; in the centre an oak desk which somehow seemed to reflect its owner's personality, dominating the rest of the room as it did. On top of various tallboys and packing cases, disorderly piles of books reached almost to the ceiling—fat, Western-published volumes interspersed with dog-eared reference works. They towered over Miss Tamura's head, as if threatening her. 'Your world is quite different from ours! This is the room of a distinguished scholar,' they seemed to say. 'You have no such learning, and shouldn't be here!' She glared back in resistance to the atmosphere of the room, and then, discarding her sandals, stepped right inside and gazed at the books, one by one, as if savouring their contents.

Seeing all these objects which had passed the years with the elegantly learned Toyoko, a grievous sense of her own inferiority welled up in Miss Tamura's bosom. 'These objects, too, have drawn into themselves the passing years as their owner's youth and beauty faded. What sort of a man was her husband, and how was their life together all those years? Was it a happy one, I wonder?' In her reverie, Miss Tamura was overwhelmed by curiosity about Toyoko's private life, and her sense of guilt vanished at last.

She moved stealthily to the desk, and spread her hands on its top. It felt cold and hard, telling her of the sternness of a scholar's life.

On the broad desktop, an old-fashioned stand for writing brushes had been pushed to one side; behind it there were several dry inkwells with pens stuck into them in confusion. There was a writing pad, its brilliant whiteness laid bare to the eye; beside it there was a neat pile, some twenty centimetres deep, of manuscripts, held in place by a marble paperweight. Immediately under the paperweight, on top of the other writings, was a sheet with the words 'Completed Manuscripts' penned in black ink.

Miss Tamura picked up the marble paperweight with both hands and placed it with great care, as if it were fragile, on the desk. She began to turn the leaves of the first manuscript, one page at a time, taking care not to disturb their order.

TITLE
'Concerning the materialisation of epicycloid curves not subject to conceptual limitations.'

This heading was written in angular lettering on squared paper, and was followed by half a page of mathematical equations made up of numerals and symbols.

Miss Tamura examined the next few pages carefully. It was after about the third page that she began to sense that something was wrong. The formation of the characters and symbols started to assume odd shapes. Then they seemed to lose shape altogether: characters were abbreviated or written as if falling apart, and were increasingly interspersed with meaningless patterns, squares, triangles, circles, and cyphers like secret letters of an incomprehensible code. Irrelevant words and phrases of gibberish began to appear, written in minute letters.

The meaningless array of letters and signs went on for fifty pages. At the very end, there appeared a final line written in Toyoko's flowing hand:

'Recorded by my husband in his place of refuge at the reception area of the boundary city.'

Miss Tamura's hands began to shake, and she was overwhelmed by astonishment. She began to wonder whether Toyoko's husband had not been insane.

The second manuscript was entirely in Toyoko's writing, but otherwise was an exact copy of the first one. The crazy title, the illogical patterns and the obscure symbols were all faithfully reproduced just as they were.

Miss Tamura began to turn the pages faster. The third manuscript was the same; the fourth too, and so on. Not the slightest change was introduced—each was just a copy of the original. She felt a malicious desire to get to the bottom of this useless labour, this pointless accumulation of meaningless data. Toyoko's bloodless face with its almost transparent, pale nose floated before her eyes, chilling her spine.

Once more she seemed to hear the flat and toneless voice of the anonymous caller on the telephone.

She gathered together the manuscripts and piled them up exactly as they had been when she had found them, replacing the paperweight on top. She realised that she had been in a panic ever since entering the room, and noticed for the first time that her sleeve had caught on one of the pens in the inkwell, upsetting it; a dark blot was spreading over a page of writing that lay on top of the desk. It was time to go, but first she must have one last careful look around the room to make sure that she left no traces of her visit. She walked around nervously, giving way to a sense of desperation. There was nothing to mop the ink up with, and even if there was it would not remove the mark on the manuscript sheets, but she could hardly throw the paper away. What could she do? Toyoko was bound to realise that someone had been in her room, but would have no way of knowing who it was. There was nothing to link her with the crime, except the master key—but then anyone could use a key, provided that they had access to it. That was it! As things stood, only the receptionists had control of the key, and its misuse could be narrowed down to them, but if it were missing—lost or stolen, say—well, some blame would fall on them for carelessness, but no one could prove that one of them had misused it!

Her mind swam. Before her eyes proceeded a vision of the faces of the residents of the apartment block. The blame had to fall on someone who had no work, who was generally at home throughout the day, someone who was unpopular or regarded with suspicion... passing the key would be just like getting rid of the Queen in the children's card game called Slippery Ann!

As if in a trance, she left the room, locking the door as she went, and hurried back to the staircase. She made her way up one flight of stairs and took off her slippers. She crept along the corridor and paused in front of the fifth door from the landing, Room 305. She looked around cautiously, and listened. No one about! Putting her ear to the door, she made sure that there was no sound from within. Just to make certain, she surreptitiously turned the doorknob; it was locked. She quickly slipped the master key into the keyhole.

Her feelings at that moment were a mixture of the relief of one who has just discarded a heavy load and the exhaustion brought on by pointless labour. She bent down and put on her slippers, noticing the while that the tally still swung on its red ribbon from the master key in the lock.

All trace of envy or sense of inferiority towards Toyoko Munekata had melted away on seeing those pitiful manuscripts, but she had no sense of triumph from laying bare her adversary's secret. She only felt as if the bonds of circumstance which had linked her to Toyoko for so long had been cut, and she was on her own in a world of darkness and aimlessness. She felt that she would have been better off in her previous ignorance. Suddenly she felt hatred and anger towards the man who had telephoned her. Why had he done it? What was his purpose? How had he known what was going on? How had he known her feelings towards Toyoko? She began to dread this unknown man, this omniscient plotter who had drawn her into his schemes. For a moment everything went black as she wondered who this person was who must have visited Toyoko's room before she did; then, with slumped shoulders she walked back along the corridor, this time quite careless of any sound her slippers might make on the floorboards.

PART FOUR

Four months before the building was moved

The case of Noriko Ishiyama

At about two am, two contrasting black shadows confronted each other in the deserted kitchen of the third floor. One was large, the other small. The large shadow kept hissing at the small one, which reared its tail, mewed grumpily and leaped up onto the windowsill. The larger shadow squatted down and foraged in the oil drum that did service as a trash-can under the sink and, finding a few fishbones, scooped them into an earthenware casserole in her lap and beat a silent retreat.

As she emerged into the dim light in the corridor, a watcher would have recognised Noriko Ishiyama, an old woman with lank dry hair and the gait of a crazy beggar-woman. She was known to the other inhabitants of the building as 'Miss Bladderwrack'—after the worn and ragged edges of the trailing skirts she always affected. Until her mid-forties, she had been an art teacher at a primary school, but had spent the last three years living on Public Assistance.

She always wore an old pair of canvas shoes with rubber soles. She found it easier to walk in them, and they had the additional advantage of silence.

Her objective on these midnight foraging trips was always the same—fishbones. She went from floor to floor, hunting down the bones and heads discarded by the other residents after their evening meals. The reason for this lay in the advice given to her by a doctor six years before. 'You must take lots of calcium,' he had said. 'For instance, eat fish heads and bones—it'll be good for you.'

This was after she had slipped and fallen on the apartment stairway while wearing Wellington boots. She had damaged her hip-bone, and had gone to see the doctor. His advice to her then had remained the guiding principle of her life. In fact, the diagnosis was erroneous, but nonetheless as a result of it Noriko had given up everything else which lent meaning to her existence, obsessively concentrating instead on the search for, the boiling and the slow mastication of, heads and bones, which she ate completely, leaving no waste.

She returned to her room just by the landing and glanced swiftly around before slipping inside. As she had learned to match her actions to those of an alley cat, she had acquired the same instincts and no longer had to spend much time in reassuring herself that she was unobserved.

The name card on her door was stained by years of dirt, but one who examined it closely could just make out the lettering against the once-white background: '305 Ishiyama Noriko'. The lettering was done by hand in an elegant italic script denoting the fact that the writer was someone with a gift for such things. In fact, until she had suffered her fall her room had been full of dainty little book-containers, dolls and paintings all reflecting in their pure lines and bright colours the childish hands that had made them; there had hardly been any space left on the walls, the shelves and the table-tops. Nowadays, however, the whole room had an unpleasant fishy smell such as no normal person could stand for more than a minute or so.

After his first diagnosis of a cracked bone, the original doctor had diagnosed nervous pains, and indeed within a year Noriko was laid up with all sorts of aches; the balance between her nerves and her resistance was soon destroyed. Her imaginary pains became real, and every day she felt them in some place or other. They became the central feature of her life, and she spent her energies trying to diagnose them for herself, looking up the names in medical books.

She visited one doctor after another, but none of them was good enough to name her illness. Instead, they would laugh and say, 'There's nothing wrong with you. It's all in the mind.'

Finally, she had had to give up her job, and with it went the necessary income to visit doctors. Thenceforth she could only discuss her ailments with her neighbours in the apartment block. She would waylay in turn anyone she could and chronicle her various aches and pains. At first, they used to listen sympathetically, but they soon found her a bore—and, worse still, began to treat her as a madwoman.

When her audience had finally vanished, Noriko Ishiyama set about creating her own little world in her room. She began to live like a mouse. After all, a mouse can't complain of its pains to human beings; a mouse makes its nest in a cupboard and only emerges at night. Indeed, on her midnight foragings she would sometimes imagine herself to be a mouse.

Her first steps on the path to a rodent's existence were to divorce herself from the everyday conveniences of human life. She switched off her gas supply at the main. She would have done the same to the electricity, removing the fuses, but she needed some light for her nocturnal existence and so changed her light bulb for the smallest she could buy, a dim light such as normal people leave on all night in the toilet.

By this cheese-paring, Noriko was able to reduce her gas and light bills, normally the smallest item in the budgets of her neighbours, to almost nothing. Also, she did her best to make do with what other people had thrown away. There was plenty for her to glean amongst the trash discarded in this large block of flats.

After five or six years of this existence, her floor was covered with other people's rubbish so that she had to pick her steps with care. In just the same way, mice too pull together all that they can find… Her storage cupboard was emptied and became her bed; all the rest of the floor space was littered and piled high with junk.

By night, the weird silhouettes of piles of cardboard boxes, newspapers and worn rags heaped in old wicker baskets were projected strangely against the walls and ceiling by the tiny low-watt lamp.

She entered the room and, picking her way with accustomed skill between the empty cans and bottles that littered the floor, made her way to a pot-bellied stove with a chimney that stood by the windowsill. She put down the earthenware casserole on top of it. The fire within glimmered faintly, fed as it was by finely shredded cardboard, newspaper balls and odd scraps of wood. She stoked it up, and a faint haze of white steam rose above the casserole which begun to bubble as the stove got hotter. There was a scratching at the door; the smell of the boiling fish scraps had reached the corridor.

'Beastly cat! Who said there'd be any for you?' she said, turning where she stood by the stove and glancing in the direction of the door. The malice in her voice was very real.

She poured a little soy-sauce into the casserole and, picking up a fish by its tail, used it to stir the brew. The silence of the room was broken by the bubbling of the pot and the sound of her sucking the fish scraps and slowly munching the bones.

The meal—if such it could be called, for it was to her more of a cure—lasted for about an hour. Then she rose from the pile of newspapers which served her as a chair and opened the sliding door of her storage cupboard. Picking up the lampstand with its trailing flex and tiny bulb, she carried it as if it was a candlestick and entered the cupboard.

Her bed made up the bottom half. The sides of the cupboard, and her bedding too, were covered with a fine white powder. It was DDT, which she sprinkled regularly, fearing that her unmade bed would otherwise become a breeding ground for insects. She wanted to keep her person, at least, clean. Her bed consisted of three under-mattresses, covered by a sheet which was so worn that the pattern of the cloth below showed through. A permanent hollow was worn in the centre, which fitted her body to her satisfaction. Above this were spread an ancient blanket with dirty edging and a heavy quilt, the stuffing of which had worked its way into the four corners, leaving nothing in the centre except the covering material. This deficiency was remedied by piling old newspapers on top of where the kapok should have been. The whole arrangement was a grubby chaos, but at least the bed was warm.

Noriko put the lamp on an old orange box by her pillow, closed the sliding door and sat on top of the bed. Now that two doors separated her from the outside world, she felt at peace—just like a mouse in its nest. She reached into the orange box and took out a tea-caddy which she up-ended, scattering its contents on the bed. An old brooch, a broken wrist watch, a magnet, a fragment of a mirror—the sort of rubbish a child would collect—such were her treasures. But amongst them was the master key with its wooden tally. She took it up, discarding the rest, and laid it on her pillow. Since finding it in the lock of her door a week before, she had taken it out and examined it every night, pondering on the reason for its having turned up there.

Just as a mouse will carefully examine the bait in a trap, occasionally touching it with its forepaws, so Noriko now inspected the key, picking it up from time to time and then replacing it on the pillow. One thing at least was clear to her: the loss of the master key having been announced on the noticeboard downstairs three days before, there was no possibility of her now returning it without incurring suspicion. But she could think of no way in which she could use the key for her own purposes.

Having adopted the life of an animal, her instincts were enough to convince her that this master key was something dangerous, boding ill-fortune for her.

PART FIVE

The stolen violin

The child was plainly bored. He stood self-confidently before the music stand, but it was clear that he had no real interest in the violin in his hands, and that his concentration was straying. When the instructor was demonstrating the correct way of playing, instead of fixing his attention on the bow he would from time to time sneak a glance at her out of the corner of his eyes.

Suwa Yatabe stood stiffly erect, her head inclined to the left the better to grip the violin under her chin and, putting all her skill into the playing, swept the bow from side to side in an exaggerated manner so that the child could understand what she was trying to teach him. Her knuckles stood out under her lacklustre skin and her fingers quivered mincingly up and down the strings; nonetheless, they seemed to dance like living things. They gave away the fact that their owner, although now condemned to play and listen to such pedestrian sounds, had once been one of the leading Western musicians of Japan, a lady violinist of breathtaking skill whose performances had often brought the house down.

The child stared at those so-correctly positioned fingers. Her little finger and ring finger pressed down the strings, whilst her index finger hopped up and down all the time, touching lightly on their surface. Her middle finger stood stiff and motionless, without ever seeming to give way to the instinct of moving. The child found this fascinating, and wanted to ask his teacher how she could accomplish this but fought back against the temptation, remembering that his mother had told him it was rude to draw attention to people's physical peculiarities.

Suwa Yatabe was aware of the child's impertinently curious gaze, but today it did not trouble her. She was herself interested in the powers of observation possessed by this highly strung boy.

Most of her pupils were children who lived nearby, those whose parents wanted them to pass the time in something more than mere play or who were sent merely because there was a violin at home on which they could practise. Mothers who could not afford a piano would give their child a small violin and send him or her off to study this fashionable instrument under Suwa. Her fees were extremely low. She had started teaching friends' children as a favour when she experienced boredom after retiring from her post as a music teacher at a girls' school; imperceptibly, as the word got around, numbers had swelled and now her apartment had more or less become a classroom. The number of pupils seemed to have reached a natural ceiling, and thereafter neither grew nor diminished: everyday, four or five children came for lessons.

Since leaving the world of the concert hall, Suwa Yatabe had suffered the chagrin of seeing the names of her former colleagues in the newspapers, and even though she was now over sixty she still felt the agonies of the frustrated artist. So, whilst teaching her pupils, she would torment herself with the thought that perhaps amongst these children there might be one in whom some latent genius lay concealed from her eyes. But at such moments the child whose practice of the necessary passages in *Holman's Primer* did so much for his mother's self-esteem, would appal the ears of the once-famous accompanist who taught him, such were the cacophonous sounds of his violin.

But the child who was with her today was different. At the very least, Suwa thought, he was better than the neighbourhood children who were her other pupils. He had been brought by his mother for the first time a week before—they lived a couple of stations away on the underground—and Suwa had detected some feeling for music in him. Of course, his accomplishment was patchy, but her long experience told her that the child had potential talent. Such a child had to be taught to the best of her ability.

'Well, listen to this, and listen carefully.' She rapped the music stand with her bow to attract the child's attention. He gazed at her timidly. 'Why does your finger not move, Teacher?'

She looked at the middle finger of her left hand. It had suddenly become paralysed when she was in her mid-thirties, at the height of her musical career, and she no longer regarded it as being part of her. She felt revive within her the terror and mortification of those days when she had first realised that the finger would no longer move. The doctors had been able to do nothing about it. They said that there was nothing really wrong with her finger, except that it would not bend. There was no medical cause that they could find.

Over the thirty years since then, Yatabe Suwa's life had been changed by the circumstance of her paralysed finger. Because of it, she had been forced to abandon her musical career and to become a mere teacher. It was only natural that she resented any questioning about it by others. On the surface, it was because she could find no answer to the question 'Why?' But deep in her subconscious she felt that she knew the answer; there it lurked, and there she preferred to leave it...

At this moment, prompted by the child's innocent question, the true answer stirred deep down in a corner of her mind. Her arm quivered as she wrestled with the problem; she tried to put it into words and failed. So once again she recited the lie, the fiction which she always produced when confronted with the question.

'Well, a long time ago your teacher had a very close friend. We always used to practise the violin together. We were just like sisters; we attended the same Academy of Music, we shared this very room. We shared everything. But one day a competition was held; the winner would get a scholarship and be sent abroad to study. We both entered the contest. As the set piece was one at which I excelled, I took first place. My friend came second; she congratulated me with a smile, but deep in her heart there was bitterness and resentment. Shortly afterwards, she left this apartment and went back to her home in the country. She took with her one single strand of my hair, and do you know what she did? She made a straw effigy of me with my hair in the centre; everyday she would take it to the garden shed and drive a nail through the middle finger of the left hand of the doll. It was because her middle finger had let her down in the competition, you see.'

The child froze. He gazed intently at Suwa's left hand, and said,

'Oh what a terrible woman she was! She was jealous of you, Teacher!'

These words, the reverse of the real truth, stirred Suwa's heart. Once again she felt the anguish of having come second in the contest. How bitter it had been for her! She wanted to blurt out the truth, to say,

'I didn't fail from want of skill. It was just that I didn't have a decent instrument. Now *she* was all right—she had an Italian violin. *Her* parents were rich, whilst I was poor. I was beaten by money…'

For thirty years, this speech had been on the tip of Suwa's tongue. Now once again it floated around her mind.

Well, she thought, as a result *she* went to Europe to complete her studies, whilst I was doomed to spend my days teaching children the fundamentals of music from *Holman's Primer*. People would call it destiny, but I can't just accept it like that. The old French Professor at the Conservatory—what was it he was always saying—'*C'est la vie, c'est la vie*'… But I'm not a fatalist—I resisted to the end. I felt sure that I would win.

She looked up at the corner cupboard that hung in her room. On top of it, covered in dust, she saw a battered old violin case. The renewed sense of defeat which had suffused her mind began to fade. She had not realised before how much the real answer to the question lay in that old violin case which had altered her whole life.

'Well, let's get back to practice. Now I've told you the reason, you'll see that I can only play with three fingers whilst you can use four. So you should be able to do better than me, shouldn't you?'

The child nodded his head. For the remaining thirty minutes of the lesson, he could not tear his eyes away from that frozen middle finger, the object of witchcraft and a curse.

When he had left, Suwa sat in a trance in the chilly classroom, which was divided from the rest of her room by a curtain.

On top of the piano there were several classical-style busts of famous composers. They glared down at Suwa, their features contorted by the agonies of genius, their hair wild and ruffled. She looked back at them, reflecting that artistic genius brings torments in its train, and that therefore much must be forgiven those who suffer it. The busts seemed to agree with her, and their expression towards her changed to one of soft forgiveness.

Ishiyama Noriko squeezed through a gap in the slate wall and made her way back into the inner garden of the building. It was five am and still half-dark, but a glow in the eastern sky and the crisp freshness of the air proclaimed that dawn was at hand. She was carrying a bottle of milk that had only just been delivered. At first it had chilled the palm of her hand, but now the temperature had risen to match her own and a light dew had formed on the glass. Certain sounds still echoed in her ears—the sound of the milkman sliding open the wooden gate, the jangle of bottles, the tinkle of the bell fixed to the gate. She was still trembling with excitement, and felt that she never wanted to take such risks again, but in her heart she knew that before the week was out she would steal another bottle of milk. Every day she would creep out as was her custom and forage for wood shavings for her stove; sometime soon she would again chance upon a freshly delivered bottle of milk that had carelessly been left within her reach. Just like a ripe fruit growing in someone's garden, hanging over the wall, waiting to be picked... But sometime she would surely be caught by a furious householder—crime always brought punishment in its wake. She thought back to the first time when she had chanced upon a milk bottle waiting for her in a delivery box with a broken lock. She had not meant to steal it at all. She had slipped her fingernail under the cap, opened the bottle and just drunk a mouthful. But so small a quantity seemed to lack flavour. She replaced the cap; it seemed to her that no one would be able to detect what she had done. All would be well, she thought, and was about to return the bottle to its box when suddenly the first rays of the sun appeared, shining directly onto the bottle in her hand. They lit up the glass revealing her fingerprints which she felt had been etched onto the bottle so that they could never be removed.

There was nothing for it but to take the bottle home. And since then, every morning, she felt the challenge of milk bottles tempting her to do the same again.

'Fingerprints.' Few other words in the language seemed to exercise such a deep hold upon her. Two years earlier, when she had picked up a man's wooden clog which had been abandoned by a dog, she had fallen into the hands of the owner, a cross-grained old gentleman who had dragged her off to the nearest policeman and accused her of theft. In order to scare her, the officer had told her that it would be a simple matter to apply a little powder to the clog, and that the fingerprints of the culprit would invariably be revealed. He had then released her with a caution, but his words had left their effect. The thought that a little

57

powder could reveal her fingerprints on anything that she had touched unnerved her so much that the words burned themselves into her subconscious. *Calcium… Fingerprints…*

The inner garden was surrounded on three sides by the brick building. There were a few flowerbeds, but apart from a small greenhouse everything was covered by straw matting in winter. There was a large incinerator with a chimney in the middle of the garden. She skirted the garden along its eastern edge and made her way to the fire escape. Her room was just next to the window giving access to the third floor, and by placing an old wooden box on the stair she could get in and out with ease and without being observed. Such was her regular custom, and today was no different. She made her way quietly up the stairs, treading the iron steps cautiously with her rubber-soled shoes, and then, when she reached the second floor, she chanced to glance back and catch sight of something she had not noticed before. On top of the incinerator was a pile of old newspapers. Their whiteness was picked out by the early-morning sun.

She made her way back down the stairway and retrieved them. They were bound neatly with string, with a sheet of cardboard at the top and the bottom to hold them in shape. The cardboard in particular would come in useful for kindling her stove. Thinking no more of the matter, she returned with them to her room. It was not until that evening that she discovered something of significance in her find.

She had spent the whole afternoon disguising the milk bottle she had stolen earlier. It was her habit to turn them into Mexican-style pitchers, or flower vases, or pot-bellied containers by covering them with papier mâché and decorating them with distemper and water-colours.

'This should do it,' she would mutter. 'Must hide the fingerprints, or else...'

By the time it was dusk, she had completed yet another little handicraft to join those she had made before. She looked at it with pleasure, wiping her paint-stained fingers on an old newspaper. Then she suddenly noticed the date on the page.

It was ridiculously old—26 January 1933. It was one of the newspapers in the bundle she had found that morning. It had been folded in four, and the edges were yellow with age.

If it had just been old, that in itself would have amounted to nothing much. But somehow the date seemed to ring a bell in her head—was it not the same as that appearing on the main noticeboard downstairs? A few days earlier, someone had put a notice there offering a high price for a newspaper of about that date. If it was, then her morning find was just like a prize-winning lottery ticket. Could her luck have taken such a turn for the better? Pausing only to wash her hands, and to smooth the paper out and press it flat between a pile of magazines, she hurried down to the noticeboard in the entrance hall. She read the notice carefully.

HIGH PRICE PAID

I am seeking a copy of any daily newspaper dated Monday, 26 January 1933. If you have such a paper, please leave it with the clerk on duty, and I will collect it and leave a good reward with her.

It was the same date! Her mind full of mixed emotions, she paced up and down the hall wondering what to do. If she received any income, she was supposed to report it to the Social Security office. What exactly was meant by 'High Price'? Until she knew, would it not be better to keep her find to herself? She felt the gaze of Miss Tojo burning into her back from where she sat behind the window and so hurried back upstairs before she could be drawn into conversation.

That night, as she lay curled up in her lair inside the cupboard, it suddenly occurred to her that she had not yet even read the paper. Why on earth would anyone want such an old newspaper? What could be its value? It wasn't as if anything of particular historical interest had happened on 26 January 1933. She got the paper out from the pile of magazines and, placing it close to the 5-watt bulb, read it with mounting emotion.

The clue was on the crime page. Under a headline *'Famous Guarnerius violin stolen'* there appeared a large photograph of a balding middle-aged foreigner dressed in a greatcoat and carrying a violin case.

The text that followed described how André Dore, having completed a five-year contract as a professor at a musical academy, was about to return home. He had been invited to give two farewell concerts in the Hibiya Concert Hall, but on returning to his hotel at the end of the first one he had opened his violin case and discovered that some-one had substituted a cheap instrument for his precious Guarnerius. It was probable, but by no means certain, that the crime had occurred in the Concert Hall. The police had no clues as to the criminal's identity. As M. Dore had gone straight back to his hotel by car, and had not let go of the violin case throughout the journey, it seemed clear that the switch had taken place during the few short minutes he had placed the case on a table in his dressing room after the concert. Of course, there were many visitors, so to have taken the violin, case and all, would have been no particular achievement in itself, but to exchange the contents of the case without being detected seemed little short of a conjuring trick, if not impossible.

What really caught Noriko's attention was one of the names at the bottom of the column. Various people had been interviewed, and amongst them was a name known to her—Suwa Yatabe, who lived on the first floor of the same apartment block. She was quoted as follows:

'It truly grieves me that my teacher should suffer this tragic loss, just as he was leaving Japan, a country he has grown to love. I hope the thief will hasten to return the violin. The only person who can get the full effect from that violin is the Professor himself.'

The article went on to say that Suwa Yatabe was the Professor's favourite pupil. As she read this, Noriko pictured Suwa in her mind as she always saw her in the corridor of the building, holding herself erect and looking every inch a musician.

And for the first time she realised why she had always felt some unconscious affinity for Suwa. It was because they were both thieves.

Noriko felt sure of it. Thirty years ago, Suwa had left her fingerprints on the violin. And how could she hope to remove them from that varnished surface? She felt an overwhelming desire to see those fingerprints for herself.

And just as earlier, Miss Tamura had been tempted to pry in the room of her classmate, Toyoko Munekata, and had turned to the master key, so now was Noriko drawn by the same magnetic force of the key which was in her possession. She took it out of the tea caddy; suddenly it had become a treasure beyond worth. She squeezed it between her fingers, examining it minutely from every angle as she imagined herself using it to enter Suwa's room. She saw herself looking at the stolen violin. And after her long day's work decorating the milk bottle, she fell asleep with these pleasant thoughts on her mind.

The unending rain which had washed the bricks of the apartment all day persisted into the evening. The damp spread up the staircase and along the corridors, making the air heavy and oppressive. Suwa Yatabe finished the last lesson of the day and led her pupil to the front porch. She opened the child's umbrella.

'Take care how you go!'

'Yes, Teacher. Bye bye!'

She watched the small figure bobbing through the rain as far as the tram stop. The cold rain occasionally blew in under the eaves, dampening her face. The chill of the stone floor crept up into her body. Age seemed to have blunted her sense of hot and cold. She felt lethargic, with no particular desire to go back to her room and make supper. After seeing the last child off every day, particularly on rainy evenings, she felt overwhelmed by an unpleasant sadness.

She pushed the heavy door to and made her way back into the apartment block. She could see Miss Tamura at her desk behind the receptionist's window. She was knitting; the needles seemed to be moving unduly slowly.

As Suwa passed the noticeboard, her eye fell on a new notice that she had not observed before. She hardly took it in until the date mentioned—26 January—struck home. This notice which so coolly required a copy of a thirty-year-old newspaper seemed to her to have a deeper motive. Clearly it was aimed at her. That was the date which had been burned into her memory for thirty years. In fact, that particular day's paper lay hidden in the recesses of her chest of drawers together with the newspapers in which she had first made her appearance on the music page all those years ago.

Her astonishment gradually changed to a blend of anger and unease. Even when the woman who lived next to her greeted her as she returned from work, Suwa didn't seem to notice. She just stood in front of the board as if blind and deaf to the world. She sensed that the great and final drama of her life had hung over her head for all those years, but had never seemed as if it was about to break until today.

She went back to her room and sat down in front of the piano. She remained there in that position all night without getting a wink of sleep. Every now and again she would look up at the old violin case on top of the three-cornered bookshelf. The famous Guarnerius had slept away the last thirty years up there. A few times each year, Suwa had taken it down and played a few notes on it, just to confirm that its tone was as beautiful as ever.

She had become quite convinced of the propriety of her actions in stealing the Guarnerius. She felt that she had been in the right, and suppressed the guilty feelings in her innermost heart by assuring herself that should the truth ever come out her defence would be artistic justification. Yet deep down she knew better. She only had to close her eyes to see again those events of thirty years before when she had acquired the violin.

Her respected teacher, André Dore, was on the brink of his departure from Japan. His final recitals were due to commence on the next day, but in spite of that he was giving Suwa her usual private lesson. She had begun to entertain sentimental feelings about him because of her admiration for him as an artist. And as she pictured once again his deep-set gentle eyes and his finely drawn high-bridged nose, she once again embarked upon the soliloquy which she had composed for herself in the role of a tragic heroine.

'When that last lesson came to an end, André Dore gazed at me. His eyes seemed at the same time to convey both passion and melancholy. I wonder—was I truly in love for the first time, or was I just pretending in order to make a pretext for getting hold of that violin I had desired for so long? He took me in his strong arms, and I closed my eyes and let him feel the smallness and softness of my body. When it was all over, I wept—I wonder why that was? Just at that moment, a car arrived to take him off for a newspaper interview; was that mere chance, or was it an intercession of God? He told me to wait there for him; after he left, I sat for a long time on the bed, and doubt gradually took possession of my mind. Did he respect me as an artist, or had he only been interested in me as a woman? It made me feel miserable. Whichever was true, in the end I could only be sad, but secretly I preferred the thought of his admiring me as a musician.

'His favourite violin, that famous Guarnerius, was just where he had left it in the room. He had not worried about it, feeling that it would be safe with me. But I left before his return, taking the Guarnerius away in my violin case… I still can't explain why I did it. Was it to hinder his departure, to have him with me a little longer? Or was it that I was overcome by the desire for a classic Italian violin? A bit of both, I suspect.

'I thought he would have to cancel his farewell recitals, but he didn't. He just carried on as if nothing had happened; as if the instrument in his hand was the Guarnerius. Neither the critics nor the audience seemed to notice that it was not so. If they did observe any poor quality in the tone, they must have put it down to the rainy weather.

'He announced the theft of his violin after that concert. Just before he left Japan, he carefully parcelled my violin, the one I had substituted for the Guarnerius, and posted it to me. It was plain he knew that I was the thief, and that he was not demanding the return of his violin. Instead, he put the blame on "some visitor unknown"; was it because he was afraid of the scandal if our brief affair came to light, or was it that he truly admired me as a violinist, or was it just that he pitied me?

'On the day he left Japan, I went down to Yokohama and stood in the crowd seeing him off. It was most unlikely that he noticed me in all that throng, but I somehow sensed in the sad glance he directed towards us a message of personal forgiveness for me. At that moment I wanted to shout out to him "I love you", but I didn't. Well, he may have forgiven me, but some months later, while trying to play the Guarnerius I noticed that the middle finger of my left hand had become paralysed. I, who had vowed to devote my whole life to playing the violin…'

With that, her soliloquy was brought to an end by her overwhelming feelings of sorrow and self-pity. She looked up once more at the violin case on the shelf. There could be no doubt that the notice asking for a copy of that day's paper, thirty years after the event, was linked with the stolen violin. She resolved to find out who it was who was now trying to track down her stolen prize.

The day after she saw the notice, she went to the receptionist's office to try and find out who was its author. Rather than attract suspicion by asking outright, she masked her intention under the guise of paying a call on whoever was on duty to pass the time of day. She reasoned that her best hope lay in picking a time when the good-natured Miss Tamura was on duty, which was from noon onward on that day.

She went down to the front office at about four pm, and, arranging her features in an unnatural smile, went to the window. Miss Tamura looked up in a startled manner; a small drop of saliva dribbled from the corner of her mouth. She had undoubtedly been catnapping again.

Suwa gradually brought the conversation round to the point. Laughing artificially, she led off: 'What a fascinating advertisement! How much would one get, I wonder, if one produced a copy of the paper?'

'Eh? Do you mean to say you have a copy?'

'No, I don't, but…'

'Nor I. It makes me wish that I'd kept my papers all these years. But old newspapers… one just throws them away after a while.'

'Has anyone come up with a copy?'

'No one so far. But there's quite a hunt going on, I can tell you. Miss Takiguchi on the fifth floor may have a copy. She's got every copy of *Woman's World* since it was first published twenty years ago. But she doesn't want to break up her collection, so she won't part with it, even on loan.'

'Ah, but that's a magazine. I can understand people keeping old magazines, but newspapers… who could imagine keeping every copy of a newspaper for all those years? And even if they did, surely they'd have donated them to a salvage drive during the war!'

'Well, the way he saw it, this is an old building and many of the residents have lived here a long time. And as she pointed out, there's one or two who are, shall we say, a bit odd, so the chances are that a copy will turn up. A bit cheeky of him to say that, I must say, even if it's true.'

'He? Who do you mean?'

'Oh, the foreigner who came and asked us to display the advertisement. He certainly wasn't stingy, though. He left this envelope to be given in exchange for the newspaper. And how much do you think was in it? Five thousand yen!'

Miss Tamura opened her desk drawer and produced a white envelope which she passed to Suwa.

'It's pretty bulky. Must all be in hundred-yen notes.'

Suwa looked at the back of the envelope, and saw the initials 'A.D.'—the same as those of André Dore, from whom she had stolen the Guarnerius! But André Dore had died fifteen years ago, in Switzerland, at the ripe age of seventy.

She tried to conceal her emotion by chatting animatedly, but realised that her face had gone as white as a sheet.

'Well, there certainly are some queer foreigners around, I must say! What on earth would he want with such an old newspaper?'

'Well, I wasn't here when he came—it was Miss Tojo. Seems he was a young man, around thirty, and handsome too—just like a movie star, it seems. He's a historian, specialising in studies of ancient Tokyo. Apparently that newspaper had a photograph of an old temple which has since been burned down.'

That was obviously a lie. If his objective was just to get a photo of the temple, the mysterious foreigner would only have to visit the newspaper publishers. So the story about the temple was just a pretext. But who on earth could the young man be? Clearly, André Dore must have had a child by some woman. For a moment, Suwa felt a pang of jealousy.

Miss Tamura went on gossiping in her usual manner. But Suwa's mind was full of other things, and she heard not a word of it all. She memorised the address on the back of the envelope before returning it to Miss Tamura. There was just a lot number in Nihonbashi, Tokyo.

'I'd love to get a look at that foreigner next time he comes.'

'Well, he says he spends a lot of time travelling, and so no one can tell when he might turn up.' Miss Tamura spoke regretfully; Suwa felt insecure at the thought of not knowing when the foreigner might appear. She resolved to go to Nihonbashi and take a look for herself.

The next day, Suwa put on one of her better kimonos, which she had scarcely had occasion to wear of late, and went to the address in Nihonbashi. It proved to be a large music shop. She bought one or two small items for her pupils, and then asked the young girl who had served her about the foreigner.

'No, there's no foreigner working here that I know of—but try the publicity department upstairs. You never know—that's the sort of place they might employ a foreigner.'

Suwa went up and asked for the manager, who proved to be a middle-aged man. She gave her name, and then very politely asked if she could contact André Dore.

The manager looked at her queerly and replied that there were no foreigners employed in the shop.

'Well, have you recently had a European ask you to hold and forward letters for him?' Suwa felt on the point of giving up.

The manager phoned all the other departments, and then regretfully informed her that there was no such case that he could discover.

Suwa, who had convinced herself of the existence of the young man called André Dore, felt bitterly disappointed and then annoyed at the trick which had been played on her. Instead of going straight home, she went to the cinema for the first time in over a year. But she could not take her mind off the foreigner who called himself 'A.D.' Her emotions were in conflict; half of her wanted to meet this man who seemed to be the son of André Dore, the other half wanted to flee him. On her way home, she bought some cakes for Miss Tamura, and gave them to her with the request that she be informed as soon as the foreigner appeared again.

But there was no word of him for several days, during which time Suwa's emotions were disturbed every time she passed the noticeboard and caught sight of the advertisement on it.

It was not until a week later that she received the letter. It seemed as if the writer knew the correct psychological moment to strike.

But before that, there was another development. Someone found a copy of the newspaper which was being sought.

On the morning of the fourth day after its appearance, the advertisement disappeared. Just as Suwa noticed this, Miss Tamura called her into the office. It was about ten-thirty; those who were going to work had all left, and there was no one around the hall.

'Well, at last someone found the paper! She brought it here last night and took the five thousand yen. She doesn't want anyone to know her name. I made sure it was the right date, and then got Miss Tojo to check too, just to be sure. It would be a terrible mistake to give all that money for the wrong paper.'

'And was there a photo of the temple in it after all?'

Well, I didn't look, to tell the truth. I just folded it up quickly and put it in a large Manilla envelope—Miss Tojo said we should take great care of it and not handle it too much in case it got damaged.

She took out the envelope from the drawer and showed it to Suwa. It was sealed.

'This is it. I hope he comes for it soon. I bet he'll be pleased.'

'Yes, but I can't help thinking of the woman who had it for thirty years. She must hoard things carefully!'

'Ah, but she's no ordinary person, that one. Her room is full of old newspapers—ah, what am I saying! I've given her away to you—you're bound to know who I mean.' Miss Tamura giggled, and went on.

'Of course, it's Miss Ishiyama, who lives on the third floor. You know, the one they call Miss Seaweed! The one with the ragged skirt, who used to be an art teacher. Well, she's receiving Public Assistance, so she's supposed to declare any income that she receives. That's why she doesn't want anyone to know. As if we would concern ourselves about her private affairs. But I wonder what she'll find to use five thousand yen on. She's a real miser, that one. Would you believe that her gas and electricity bills are next to nothing?'

The image of the beggarly Noriko Ishiyama floated into Suwa's mind. That old miser had spent the last four days going through all the newspapers in her room in order to get her hands on five thousand yen. And at last she had found it; had she read it, and, seen the article about the violin? Well, even so, it didn't matter. Suwa felt that Noriko Ishiyama's finding the paper bore no direct connection to her own problem.

'But please don't tell a soul, Miss Yatabe, I beg of you—it wouldn't do to have it get around.'

Miss Tamura smiled sweetly at Suwa. Clearly she wanted to strengthen the relationship between the two of them. Suwa thereby realised that she need have no fear that her secret—her link with the old newspaper—was known to either of the receptionists. Thereafter, her only worry was Noriko Ishiyama, and she felt a slight frisson every time she passed her in the corridor.

During that week, apart from Noriko having found the newspaper and claiming her five thousand yen, nothing out of the ordinary occurred. The foreigner did not turn up to collect the paper. Nonetheless, Suwa felt a sense of foreboding. Then the letter arrived, brought to her one afternoon by a pupil who had been given it to deliver by the front office. Suwa put it on the piano and tried to conduct the lesson as if nothing out of the ordinary had occurred. But she was more than usually severe with her pupil during that lesson, torn as she was by the desire to leave her duties for just a moment to attend to her private business. That square white envelope seemed to dance before her eyes wherever she looked, threatening her and disturbing her concentration. Suwa's name and address were written with unexceptionable penmanship; when she had received the envelope from the hands of the child, she had sneaked a glance at the back, and sure enough, in the space reserved for the sender's name there appeared the initials 'A.D.' Well, the anticipated had at last occurred; she felt half resigned to the fact that her fate had caught up with her, half afraid, and altogether disturbed. The thirty-minute lesson period seemed to drag on and on. At last it came to an end; she saw the pupil off and then hurried back to her room and tore the envelope open. There was just one sheet of notepaper inside; the message was written in perfect Japanese.

Dear Madam,

Thank you for going to the trouble of sending me the newspaper dated 26 January 1933.

Further to this, I would really like to discuss with you the matter of the musical instrument.

72

I shall wait at the entrance of the Hibiya Concert Hall
from four pm on 12 February. I shall wear a red carnation in
my buttonhole.

It will give me great pleasure if you would be so good as
to meet me there.

A.D.

The handwriting could not have been that of a foreigner;
some Japanese must have written it at A.D.'s request. But
what was the meaning of the reference to the newspaper,
the insinuation that Suwa had sent it to him? He hadn't
come to the apartment block; instead, he proposed a
meeting at the Hibiya Hall. Why? And why did the sender
shelter behind initials, instead of having the grace to reveal
his full name and details? It was all beyond her. There
was just one possibility that occurred to her; dismiss it as
she might, she could not drive it entirely from her mind.
Perhaps someone else living in the apartment block had
sent a copy of the newspaper using her name. But she
could think of no possible motive for anyone doing such
a thing. Nonetheless, she could not entirely rule out the
possibility.

She wondered what attitude she should adopt when she
met the foreigner. Even more important was the question
as to whether she should meet him at all. The more she
racked her brains, the harder the problem became.

André Dore had publicly forgiven her, and the question of theft no longer arose. But now it was as if the case
had been reopened after a lapse of thirty years, and the
sole witness to her intentions and his forgiveness was
no longer of this world. She was afraid, but there was no

alternative to going to Hibiya Hall at the appointed time, on 12 February—the very next day.

The corridor on the ground floor was a gloomy place even in the middle of the day, and when the weather outside was overcast or when it was sleeting it was necessary to turn on the lights to find one's way around.

Noriko came out of the washroom and made her way along the passage, pausing for a few seconds at each light switch. She turned the light on for a moment, to make sure she knew where the next switch was, and then flicked it off again. In this manner, she progressed slowly towards Suwa Yatabe's room, pausing every now and again to make sure that no one was coming. If she had perchance been observed by any of the other residents, the chances were that they would find nothing strange in her behaviour, knowing her eccentricity as they all did.

She had carried out this procedure for the last four or five days, on the pretext of visiting the downstairs toilet. Every time she had crept up to Suwa's door and listened carefully for a while. Sometimes she had heard music, or rather attempts at music shrill enough to set her teeth on edge; at other times, she heard Suwa's voice, usually scolding her pupil. Once or twice, she had bumped into Suwa making her way to the front hall, a shopping basket in her hand. But she did not feel that the length of absence involved in a mere shopping trip would give her long enough for her purpose.

Ever since finding the old newspaper on top of the incinerator, Noriko had been consumed by the desire to enter Suwa's room, find the stolen violin, and ascertain the state of the thief's fingerprints on it. So every night she would get out the master key, the loss of which had caused old Miss Tamura so much trouble, and arouse herself with the thought of using it for her purpose.

'Like me, she's haunted by the thought of her finger-prints. All those years ago… Maybe, just as I only wanted to try a mouthful of milk, she wanted to play that famous violin just once.' Such were her thoughts as she massaged her aching thighs. Suwa was like her, a victim of similar misfortune. But in spite of this feeling of Noriko's, she sensed that when they bumped into each other, Suwa gave her the same suspicious glance as the other residents did.

Somewhere behind her she heard a door grating open. She felt sure that it was Suwa's door. This was her third sally into the ground-floor corridor that morning, and so far she had heard not a sound from Suwa's room. Plainly, she had no pupils that day. Noriko pretended to be looking for something she had dropped on the floor, meanwhile stealing a glance back down the corridor.

Suwa was quite plainly dressed to go out. Instead of the shopping basket she had a handbag; in place of the slip-ons she wore to go around the neighbourhood, she had on a pair of high-heeled shoes. She seemed to be lost in thought as she locked her door and made her way towards the exit. She paused for a few words with the receptionist and left the building. She did not seem to have noticed Noriko.

The sky was slate grey, and seemed pregnant with sleet or rain. Noriko, who was following Suwa at a distance, felt a piercing chill around her shoulders; she shivered, and drew the lapels of her jacket closer across her breast.

Suwa was plainly deep in thought. She stepped onto the pedestrian crossing without noticing that the light was red, and was shouted at by a taxi driver who had to pull up suddenly. The wind whipped up the skirts of her long winter coat, revealing for a moment her spindly legs. Then the light changed, and she hurried across the road.

Noriko watched her go, and almost lost sight of her in the throng. Then she saw her again; without casting a glance behind her, Suwa jumped onto a tram. It was crowded with cheerful and bustling children, for the school day had just ended. Pushed here and there by the young students, Suwa, as was her wont, yet stood as stiff as a ramrod amongst the seething mass of people.

Noriko stayed hidden behind a telegraph pole until the tramcar had vanished into the distance. She wondered where Suwa was going. It didn't look to her as if she would be back all that soon. Noriko turned round and made her way back as fast as her strange prancing gait, which seemed designed to protect her loins from some attack, would permit her. Her long tattered skirts brushed against the ground, sometimes fluttering in the wind. Her jacket only came down to her elbows; underneath it she was wearing a grubby blouse. Her lank, dry hair was disordered in the wind. Passers-by turned to stare at her retreating figure.

Miss Tojo was sitting at the reception desk, her head bowed over a book. Noriko wandered slowly down the ground-floor corridor, taking in her surroundings cautiously. There was no one around; this was her chance to enter Suwa's room. She slipped her hand under her blouse and withdrew the precious master key from its hiding place between her flaccid breasts. She felt the warmth of her own body in the metal.

She opened Suwa's door and slipped into the room. She stood in the tiny entrance space which opened directly onto the room, which she took in in one glance. Suwa must have had the gas stove on until just before leaving; Noriko felt the warm air brush against her cold cheeks. She stole one more swift glance down the corridor, and then closed the door and locked it from the inside, leaving the key in the lock. She didn't even bother to slip off her canvas shoes, but gazed around the room in wonder. The main items of furniture were a piano and a standard lamp. They had both been articles of some quality in their day but now had a faded and worn look. The large lampshade was covered in blotches and stains so that it looked like some strange map. Two curtains hung across the room, dividing it; beyond them she could see an unmade bed, the covers of which were thrown half back. Everything about the room spoke of the occupant having left in a great hurry.

She decided to begin her search in the living half of the apartment. Discarding her shoes, but carrying them with her, she entered the room.

The first focus of her attention was the piano. There were three uncased violins on top of it but clearly, from their size, they were children's instruments. There didn't seem to be anywhere where a violin case could be hidden.

She went through the curtain into the inner half of the room. There, on the bedside table, she found a black violin case which seemed to have been put down untidily without any particular concern. She wrapped an old rag around her finger and opened the catch of the case. The violin shone sombrely in the gloom. Her feeling was that both the case and the instrument reeked of humanity, suggesting that both were in regular use. Although she knew nothing of musical instruments, and had no way of telling the stolen Guarnerius from any other violin, she instinctively felt that this was not it.

But she did somehow sense that the stolen violin was not far away. She put the case back on the side table and peered under the bed. The space was occupied by empty cardboard boxes, odd shoes, rolled-up blouses and stockings, all covered with dust, but there was no sign of a violin case. The only remaining hiding places were the wall cupboard and the wardrobe. She looked inside the wardrobe first; as soon as she opened the doors, she was overpowered by a strong smell of mothballs issuing from the dated and faded dresses and gowns which must have been designed long ago for appearances on the concert platform. The wall cupboard was full of dress boxes and willow baskets such as Japanese clothes are stored in. She went through them all, but to no avail. She had already spent nearly twenty minutes in her search, and felt on the verge of giving up. She went over to the piano, opened the lid, and peeped inside. There was nothing to see but the dusty strings. She looked again at the violin on top of the piano. It told her nothing.

She went and sat down on the small chair which was obviously used by the students, and took one final look around the room. Surely she had overlooked nothing? The violin could not be in this room.

She heard footsteps outside, and started up towards the window. Whoever it was went past the door and further down the corridor. But at that moment, as she gazed fearfully towards the door, she caught sight of a small triangular shelf, set high up in the corner, on which there reposed a black violin case. It lay there, covered like everything else in the room with a film of dust, showing signs of long neglect. It had to contain the Guarnerius. She dragged her chair over to the entrance and stood on it. She could easily reach the violin case; once again covering her fingers with rags, she gripped the case and took it down from the shelf. Her nostrils tingled, sensing the proximity of stolen property. Hardly daring to breathe, and holding her discovery high above her head, she carefully stepped down from the chair and laid the case on the floor. Her trembling hands swiftly sought the catch—but it was locked! She tried rapping the fastening to see if it would loosen but, decrepit as the case seemed, it would not yield to her efforts. Suwa must have taken the key with her when she went out. There was no point in searching for it. Her blood raced as she experienced both dread and an overwhelming desire to see inside the violin case. The latter emotion proving the stronger, she stood up with the intention of looking for something with which to force the lock.

At that very moment, she heard footsteps in the corridor. They stopped outside the door, and there was a grating sound as a key was pushed into the lock. Suwa had come back! Noriko almost fainted from fright.

The master key, which she had left in the lock on the inside of the door, began to move under the pressure from outside. If she did nothing about it, the key would be pushed out of the hole and Suwa would be able to enter the apartment.

But what could she do? Hypnotised by dread, she could not even think. For if she was discovered in Suwa's room, she would be branded as a thief and at the very least forced to leave the apartment block. A hot feeling on her inner leg aroused her; without noticing, she had passed water.

There was only one route of escape—the window. She raced over and unwound the catch, throwing the two leaves of the window outwards. She looked down; the ground was only about one metre below her, and there was no one in the inner courtyard. She looked back at the door; the master key had not yet yielded to the siege. Suwa was now rattling the knob impatiently. The Guarnerius case lay where she had left it on the floor. Now that her escape route lay open, and with no sign that Suwa would be able to effect entrance very quickly, she calmed down and realised that she had left her canvas shoes in the room and that also it would be a pity just to leave the violin behind after all her efforts.

There were sounds of other people gathering in the corridor. Miss Tojo's shrill voice could be heard amongst them. There was no time to spare. Noriko acted as if in a trance, seizing up the violin case and her shoes and racing to the window. As she climbed out, her bedraggled skirt caught on the window catch and ripped as she tumbled to the earth. Without pausing to look around, she raced barefoot across the muddy yard; and slipped and fell. The violin case flew from her grasp and struck the brick-built incinerator house, suffering severe damage. She picked it up again and gazed wildly around the courtyard looking for somewhere to hide. With so many people around, she could not use the fire escape as was her normal custom. It looked as if she was cornered.

But there was one hiding place available to her—the incinerator. She wrenched open the iron doors and, pushing the violin case in first, crawled in after it. The interior was much wider than appeared from the size of the doors. Provided she was not discovered, she could remain hidden until nightfall and then make her escape. She only had to put up with cramped conditions for an hour or so. The incinerator had not been used for some time, and the recent rainfall had turned the half-burned paper and rubbish inside into a black paste which was extremely unpleasant to the touch. She wiped her feet with her rags and put on her canvas shoes.

After a while, she peeped out through a crack in the doors. She could see some of the windows on the lower two storeys of the building—but not the window of Suwa's room. Doubtless people were clustered around that window, gazing into the courtyard. Indeed, she felt as if every window must conceal a pair of eyes gazing directly at the incinerator. She crouched in the dark, hardly daring to breathe and clasping the violin case to her breast.

Thirty minutes passed in this way, with no sign of anyone coming into the courtyard. She felt a strong desire to uncurl herself and have a look at the violin. Her eyes were now accustomed to the dark; indeed, what with various cracks in the structure and the open chimney, the interior of the incinerator was quite light. She felt around in the cinders and found a rusted five-inch nail. She tried to force open the lock of the case with it, but to no avail.

Then she noticed that the hinge had been distorted in the fall. She slipped the nail under it and prised it open in no time at all. The lid then came apart from the case with ease.

The violin lay there, its paint cracked in places. Not one string remained unbroken. There was a hole in the belly of the instrument, through which she could see a slip of brown paper pasted to the inside of the back. Could this indeed be the famous Guarnerius violin?

'Poor violin,' she thought. 'Just to cover up her finger-prints, she scrubbed your paintwork and stuck on a piece of paper to hide the traces.'

She put the violin down, and conjured up a vision of Suwa's face covered with the fingerprints of guilt. They were two of the same tribe, she and Suwa.

Her long-awaited object at last achieved, Noriko suc-cumbed to the mental and physical exhaustion of the hunt. She fell asleep in the incinerator, the violin cradled in her arms. She awoke with a sneeze some while later, chilled to the bone. She put the violin back in its case, and hid it carefully in the back of the furnace.

Outside, it was pitch dark. A few lights yet shone in the windows as Noriko crept to the fire escape and made her way back to her room.

The evening concert had begun half an hour before. Suwa Yatabe was standing in the cold winter dusk outside the Hibiya Hall, gazing at the gloomy park. Occasionally, the sound of music within was wafted to her in the wind, arous-ing the bright memories of her past, only to fade as her career had faded.

It was well past the time of her appointment, but the foreigner who called himself 'A.D.' was nowhere to be seen. But she could not bring herself to give up and leave, hoping against hope that he would finally turn up.

The square in front of the Concert Hall was bathed in the pale light of mercury lamps. Apart from the occasional latecomer hurrying into the Hall, it was more or less deserted. A uniformed driver got out of a parked limousine, but it was only to wipe the window before retreating back into the car.

Suwa stamped her feet to keep the cold at bay, and from time to time moved from one pillar to the next.

A car turned in off the road, sweeping the square with its baleful headlights. It crunched across the gravel and came to a stop. A foreigner, wearing a long greatcoat turned up at the collar, got out and paid the driver. She could not see his face clearly, but he turned towards her and came bounding up the steps. Suwa stepped out from behind the pillar which had been hiding her, her heart pounding like a drum. But then she noticed that he was wearing glasses, and her heart sank.

The foreigner did not enter the Concert Hall but stood near her looking around as if seeking someone. He looked at her, and as their eyes met he seemed to be laughing. Suwa was just about to speak to him when a young girl rushed out of the Hall and greeted the foreigner effusively. They linked arms and went inside, leaving a disappointed Suwa outside.

Suwa realised that it was now three hours past the appointed time, and that there was really no use waiting any longer. But she could not tear herself away from the pillar by which she was standing.

She had arrived twenty minutes late. She had come by tram because she felt that an hour was plenty of time to allow. She had changed trams at K Street, and thus escaped the rumbustious school children who had trodden all over her in the other tram. Gazing out of the window, she had passed the time with memories of long ago. For whatever other changes had occurred, the trams were still the same. The streetcar rolled on, stopping and starting, drawing nearer to her destination. Her thoughts turned towards the meeting that lay ahead; what sort of stance should she take towards the foreigner?

The tram came to the area full of old ministerial offices built in red brick. They soothed her eyes and her heart. She realised that the desire that had caused her to steal the violin was now dead. She was sixty-five years old, and one of her fingers would not move properly. There was no possibility of her playing the Guarnerius ever again.

The tram stopped, and an old woman of about Suwa's age got on, leading her grandson by the hand. They took a vacant seat, and gazed out of the window together. Seeing them, anyone would think what a charming and happy pair they made, but Suwa was never one to be moved by such warm emotions. Even when she was a schoolgirl, and the class had been taken to the zoo, she had not been as enchanted as her form-mates by the sight of a mother bear playing with her cub. She was more interested in the solitary male bear pacing to and fro in the next cage.

But for once her mood was different, and the sight of the old lady taking care of her grandchild did not annoy her. If this Mr A.D. was really André Dore's son, then, she decided, she would return the Guarnerius to him without a word. How happy that would make him!

There was still half an hour to go to the appointed hour of her meeting—ample time to go back to her apartment and collect the Guarnerius without further ado. She alighted at the next stop. She took a taxi, and reached her apartment in less than ten minutes, never dreaming that during her brief absence someone else had stealthily entered her room. So she wasn't particularly disturbed at first when the key refused to fit into its hole, putting it down to her hastiness. Until someone had brought Miss Tojo from the reception desk, it didn't even cross her mind that there was another key in the hole, but on the inside of the door.

'Hullo! Anyone in there? Who's there?'

Miss Tojo rattled the doorknob and pushed with all her might as she shouted, but there was no reply.

'Why don't we get in through the window?' panted Miss Tamura, who had also come to the scene as quickly as her legs would carry her.

'But it'll be locked from the inside,' replied the woman who lived three doors up. She spoke as confidently as if it were her room. Suwa could do nothing but stand and gape as the debate raged round her. Finally it was agreed that the best thing to do would be to poke out the key with a piece of wire, but in practice this was not as easy as it had seemed and took a full five minutes. When at last they got the door open, there was no particular sign that anyone had been inside apart from the fact that the window was open. Suwa immediately looked up at the top of the corner cupboard and her heart sank. The

Guarnerius, which had reposed there for so many years, was gone.

'Good heavens above! It's the missing master key!' exclaimed Miss Tamura, holding it up for all to see.

'Whoever it was got in here using the master key, which she had to leave behind in her haste to escape when Miss Yatabe came back. And if we find out who that person is, we shall also know who stole the master key,' said Miss Tojo in an icy tone of voice.

Suwa went to the window and looked out into the garden. Not a soul was to be seen. The thief who had made good her escape was clearly a fellow resident of the building.

'Well, we'd better call the police,' said Miss Tamura. But Suwa could not afford to waste any more time. It was imperative that she get to Hibiya on time, and she had already spent twenty minutes in the apartment since getting back there.

'No, it really won't be necessary. Nothing is missing.'

'That's all very well and good, but it isn't nice to think that there's someone amongst us who is capable of stealing the master key and breaking into any room she likes. However, I suppose it's all right now we have the master key back,' reassured Miss Tamura.

'Very well,' said the floor representative on the residents' committee. 'But I insist that we have a full committee meeting first thing tomorrow to thrash this matter out.'

And with that, the crowd began to dissolve and so permitted Suwa to hurry off to her meeting. Now, more than ever, she felt she had to meet this foreigner who called himself 'A.D.' There was no time to be lost, so she took a taxi rather than the streetcar. She urged the driver on, but to no avail; by the time she reached Hibiya, it was twenty minutes after the appointed time for her meeting.

Unfortunately, her arrival coincided with the end of the matinee performance and the emerging crowd streamed down the steps, and she was caught up in the jostle and buffeted from side to side. At last the mass thinned out a little, and Suwa peered anxiously around, seeking a man wearing a red artificial flower in his buttonhole, but he was nowhere to be seen. The crowd melted away until Suwa was left standing on her own, but she still couldn't bring herself to go home. She stood in the dusk gazing vacantly at the darkening park.

After two more hours, the audience for the evening performance began to arrive. She stood gazing mechanically at the lapels of the people around her, but everyone was wearing heavy overcoats which hardly seemed suitable for a red artificial flower.

By now she was cold and tired, and felt as if her body was being sucked into the hard concrete under her feet. Nevertheless, she refused to give up. The violin itself had ceased to concern her—all she wanted was to meet the young man whom she imagined to be the spitting image of her long-dead teacher—André Dore's shadow on earth, as it were.

She took little strolls to try and keep warm, always returning to the pillar, but by now there was nobody else around. At the entrance, the girl who had been checking tickets stood shivering slightly and gossiping with a friend. Suwa determined to stay on to the bitter end.

But when the concert was over, and the emerging audience once again engulfed her, drawing her body along with it, she realised at last that she had to go home. The thought of returning alone to her room, with no one to speak to, overcame her with sadness. Solitude and loneliness were her lot in life. If only she had borne a child... But she had only had one chance to do that in all her life, and that was on that evening with André Dore. She thought back to what had happened then, reliving every moment, until her cheeks flushed with embarrassment. Whilst in his arms, she had called out again and again how she was afraid of becoming pregnant. She really felt that she was going to conceive, and when it was over she kept repeating one word over and over again. 'Baby. Baby. Baby.' André Dore took her gently in his arms and cradling her face between his hands reassured her in soft whispers.

And now, thirty years later, those moments were rekindled and Suwa remembered what he had said. Once again she heard his nasal French in her ear—'I cannot give you a child—it's impossible for me to do so.'

And now the force and meaning of those words came back to her. *I cannot give you a child—it's impossible for me to do so.*

The realisation made her lose touch with her surroundings, almost as if she was about to faint. The dark woodlands of the park, the hard concrete beneath her feet, the steps, the pillar, all seemed to fade away before her eyes as at last she understood the final meaning of what the Frenchman had said. He could have no child; therefore, no child of his could possibly be alive; now, more than ever, she was all alone in the world.

She began to sob, and made her way down the long stairway, choking back her tears and wondering how she could face the loneliness of her room that night. Suwa Yatabe turned away all her pupils for the next week on the grounds of ill-health. When they saw her pale drawn face peering round the door, they were at first astonished, but then their feelings gave way to jubilation at the thought of having a break from music practice.

It took her a full seven days to get over her experience outside the Concert Hall. She pondered long and painfully over how to unravel the tangled skein of her life. At last she realised that the first step must be to put the mysterious foreigner out of her mind. Once she had made up her mind on that point, she began to feel slightly better, and was at last able to get up from her bed. Going to open the window she discovered a torn piece of black cloth caught in the latch, of a colour and type that could belong to none but Noriko Ishiyama.

The mere sight of that small black scrap of evidence brought to Suwa's mind the vision of Noriko prowling past her door. For there was no one else in the apartment block who still wore so outmoded a thing as a skirt made of black crêpe de Chine. From the shape of the tear, too—a clean, right-angled rip enclosing the jagged and frayed hem of Noriko's unique costume—she could be sure of the owner's identity. And last but not least there was the musty, beggar-woman's smell—final proof of Noriko's guilt.

She had no way of knowing why Noriko had entered her room and stolen the violin, nor of how she had come to possess the master key which she had left behind in her flight. She could only imagine that Noriko had scented the violin's presence in her room through reading that old newspaper article.

She no longer minded so much that Noriko had taken the Guarnerius. For that tramp-like old woman could hardly have any use for the instrument; all Suwa needed to do, she reasoned, would be to confront her with her guilt and secure the prompt return of the violin by means of a few well-chosen threats.

The next morning, after taking a late breakfast, Suwa made her way upstairs to Noriko's room and knocked on the door. There was no reply, but she refused to be put off and kept up a steady knocking until at last the door was opened. Noriko Ishiyama had plainly just risen from her bed; her hair was in disarray and a little saliva was dribbling from the corner of her mouth. She stood stunned by the sight of her unexpected visitor, whose relentless glare she could feel penetrating beyond her, seeking out the mountainous pile of old papers and cardboard boxes in her room behind her.

Suwa paused to take in the scene, astonished by the sheer volume of Noriko's collection, before thrusting the torn cloth in front of Noriko's eyes.

'Yours, I think?'

Her look seemed to forestall any possibility of denial, but nonetheless Noriko replied, 'I've no idea. I know nothing about it.'

'It's no good pretending innocence! That filthy skirt of yours got caught in the window while you were escaping—look, you can see where it tore!'

Suwa pointed down to a jagged rent in the hem of Noriko's skirt.

'That's an old tear! I didn't tear it in your room, whatever you say!'

'What's the point of lying about it? I know perfectly well that you broke into my room and stole the violin. But so far, I'm the only one who knows, so if you'll just give it back to me, I'll forget all about it, and no one else need ever know. But if you don't, then I'm going to tell everybody that it was you who broke into my room, you who stole the master key. Then you'll be kicked out of your room for sure!'

Noriko just ignored her. She stood tight-lipped and pale, saying not a word.

'Come on—say something! You'd better—this whole room of yours is full of stolen goods by the look of it.'

'How dare you say that? What proof have you got, to come here and speak of stolen goods? You're a fine one to talk, I must say! What a nerve you've got! *You* stole a famous violin, and then come accusing me of theft! I suppose you think you can treat me like this because I'm on Social Welfare? Well, you'd better think again!'

As Noriko spoke, she got more excited, and her body began to tremble violently as her voice rose to a shout. Suwa began to feel that the tables were being turned; the fortress of her own righteous wrath was being battered by Noriko's anger.

'Stop trying to evade the issue!' she replied. 'If that's going to be your attitude, I'll just have to report you to the police.'

'Oh really? You just try that and see! They'll find your fingerprints on the violin, and then what will you say? Now get out, and don't come back, or I'll scream so that everyone can hear!'

And with that she slammed the door in Suwa's face. Suwa seethed with impotent rage, but could do no more than retrace her steps back to her own room, muttering curses as she went. 'Dirty insect! Filthy caterpillar!'

Once back in her own room, she pondered how best to recover the violin. In her mind's eye she saw the heaped pile of rubbish in Noriko Ishiyama's room. Without doubt, her precious Guarnerius lay buried somewhere in the middle of that pile.

She thought of starting a fire. If that mass of old paper caught light, Noriko would have to run for her life. And everyone else would be absorbed in rescuing their most valued possessions and fleeing the building. Under cover of the confusion, she might be able to recover the violin. Even if she didn't, at least she'd have the pleasure of having punished Noriko. Having got this thought into her mind, Suwa set about working out a means to implement her plan. She thought of a way of setting fire to the newspapers in Noriko's room.

Many years before, when she was still a mere child, Suwa had lived in the country next to a fruit farmer. She remembered how she used to watch her neighbour kill off the insects on the trees. He used to take a long bamboo pole, and fit some benzine-soaked rags to the tip. Lighting this torch, he would burn off the insects before they could harm his cherry trees. In her rage, she could think of no better way of dealing with 'that caterpillar'.

And so it came about that a day or so later, at about three-thirty am, Suwa put the necessary materials for fire-raising into a bag and taking up a thin bamboo about a yard long made her way back to Noriko's room. In the silence of the night, even the slightest sound carried, so that it seemed even more likely to awaken suspicion by trying to muffle her steps. So perversely she took no precautions, other than wearing a pair of straw sandals, to conceal the sounds of her progress. She flushed the toilet on the landing of her floor and, under cover of that sound, made her way up to the floor above.

There was no light to be seen from within Noriko Ishiyama's room. She pressed her ear to the door, but could hear no sound. Suwa squatted down in the corridor and began to unpack the contents of her paper bag. She took out a small bundle of kindling wood, and some torn scraps of rag, and placed them on the floor. She soaked the rags in benzine and then wound them round the kindling wood so that the final result looked like a lollipop. Taking the bamboo, she pushed against the fanlight above the door, until it opened a few inches. As she had expected, it was not locked from within. She let it close again, and then looked around carefully, holding her breath and listening. There was not a sound to be heard, and nothing untoward apart from the strong smell of the benzine. She struck a match; the sound grated in the silence. Then she applied it to the rags, which flared up, lighting her immediate surroundings and throwing a dim light beyond. She bided her time while the kindling wood caught fire, opening the fanlight once again with the bamboo pole and counting up to ten before she threw the burning torch into Noriko's room. She let the fanlight close again, and paused to await the results of her action, but could see no glimmer of light from within. She walked slowly back to the toilet on the floor below. The window was set at an angle so that she could see the side of the courtyard overlooked by Noriko's room. It took her a minute or so to get there, and then with careful deliberation she opened the frosted glass window and looked out. Now she would know if her scheme had worked.

A deep red glow could be seen in Noriko's window. Suwa had remained icy calm throughout the preparation and execution of her plan, but now for the first time she felt her flesh creep. She rushed out of the toilet and, reaching the landing of the floor above, tried to shout 'Fire! Fire!' with all her might, but her vocal chords seemed paralysed.

Just at that moment, she tripped over a small, round black object, and the shock overcame her paralysis. The cat, for such it was, reared up and hissed before escaping. Suwa beat at the nearest door to hand and then, hearing screams from a room down the passage, turned and fled back to her own room as if in a trance. Her teeth chattered, and she had lost control of her senses. She threw herself down and burrowed between her bed-covers without bothering to undress. After a minute or so she heard a siren approaching in the distance. She covered her head with the pillow and remained, trembling, in her bed.

After an hour, the red dawn light filtered into her room through the window. She heard the bustle subside and the last fire engine drive away in the street below, its bell still ringing. But still the building echoed with the coming and going of many feet.

She put on a coat and made her way to the confusion that raged on the floor above.

The corridor outside Noriko Ishiyama's room was crowded by other residents of the building, many of them from other floors who were already dressed to go to work. A small group was standing outside Noriko's room, peering in. The floor of the passage was covered with the drenched ashes of burned quilts and clothing. Everywhere there was the stench of scorched cloth and cardboard.

The interior of Noriko's room was a swamp of burnt rubbish, on top of which, here and there, an empty milk bottle floated. The walls and ceiling were coated with small scraps of charred cardboard. Suwa peered over the shoulders of the crowd, dreading what she might see But there was no sign of a burnt corpse, nor was there any trace of a violin case.

'They took her away in an ambulance,' said someone knowingly. 'She slept in the cupboard, you know, so she was very badly burned before they could get her out. The whole room was full of old paper, and it went up like a bonfire. The firemen said that it's sheer madness to use a pot-bellied stove in such conditions—it's bound to lead to a fire in the long run.'

It seemed that no one suspected the real cause of the fire. Suwa went back to her room. But it was a long time before she could overcome her dread of a sudden call by the police. She stayed behind locked doors, and gradually her pupils ceased to come.

Noriko Ishiyama's life was saved, but she spent a long time in hospital. Miss Tamura opined that she would have to spend the rest of her days in an old people's home.

Suwa Yatabe abandoned all hope of ever seeing the Guarnerius again.

The violin case lay under the pile of ashes in the incinerator, just as Noriko had left it. From time to time, people kindled fires above it, never dreaming that it was there.

PART SIX

Three months before the building was moved

The case of Yoneko Kimura

That morning, as was her unvaried custom, Yoneko Kimura left her room at precisely ten-thirty, holding a letter and fifty yen in cash.

When she had first retired from her post as a teacher of the Japanese language at the Takebayashi Girls' School, she hadn't known what to do with the time which suddenly hung so heavily on her hands. After a while, she began to devise ways of occupying herself.

At first, she used to go out at eight-thirty am, just as in the old days of her employment, and stroll to Ikebukuro. Once there, she would visit the cinema at the specially reduced price for the morning show and then wander around one or other of the department stores. This certainly killed time, but after a short while she had to give up this routine for two reasons.

First of all, it cost money—more than she could really afford. She had to pay to go into the cinema, and after window-shopping in the department store she would buy some hot sweet drink or other to restore her energy, or to prevent her throat from drying. (In reality, she was really fond of such drinks, and so these pretexts were rationalisation.)

Then in addition, mixing with the busy crowds brought home to her more than ever her real sense of loneliness. It even seemed better to stay in her little concrete cell of a room, contemplating whatever the future might have in store for her, and for a while she tried that. At least she could give her imagination free rein, and at least it was better than sitting on the department store benches by the urns where green tea was served free, and where she suffered the pangs of looking about her at the other old women of her age who also gathered in such places.

After confining herself to her room for a month, she became listless and lost her appetite, and so took to going out again just for the sake of the exercise. This time, she went in the opposite direction from Ikebukuro. She felt like a convalescent after a long illness, viewing the outside world with a fresh vision. Every few hundred yards along the way there was a red postbox; these became landmarks of her daily voyage, identifying for her the distance she had gone and how far she still had to go. And so it came about that day after day she would, almost subconsciously, take in the presence of the postboxes... until one day a thought suddenly struck her.

After all, postboxes were not just set up along the road as landmarks or as milestones. Why shouldn't she use them for their proper purpose? Why not write letters to people?

Going back to her room, she opened her closet and got out the old graduation magazines from her former school. They made a heavy pile on her desk.

Her former pupils were almost too numerous to count. She determined to write to each in turn, one per day, starting with the earliest ones and working through them in alphabetical order. It wouldn't matter if she got no replies.

And in that instant of decision, the purposeless emptiness of her recent existence fell away and she felt a deep sense of satisfaction as she thought of the task which would occupy the hours and days ahead.

Thenceforth, not a day passed but she wrote a letter to one of her former pupils. Generally, she wrote in the evening, spending about four and a half hours on the task. When the letter was complete, she would fold it carefully and put it in the addressed envelope, but she would not stamp it. She would leave it on her desk and go to bed. She got a particular satisfaction from once again employing the skills of her former profession, taking the due care in composition to be expected of a teacher of Japanese.

When she got up the next morning, she never re-read the letter. She would instead open the graduation list and underline the name of her latest addressee in red ink, and number it in sequence. This businesslike procedure gave her the satisfaction and security of routine. Then she would set out on her morning walk. She would stop at the small tobacconist at Otsuka Nakamachi and buy twenty Shinsei cigarettes and a ten-yen stamp. She would then stamp the letter and post it in a different box every day; the box, too, was predetermined according to the order of its position along her route. As for the rest of her day, it was spent in her room, so that her life was structured by the actions of writing and posting her daily letters. Her mind was concentrated, each new day, upon the former pupil to whom she was writing. First she would repeat the name of the girl over and over again until the image of her arose in her mind like a bubble of gas long trapped at the bottom of a swamp. At that instant, she could once more see her correspondent as she had been all those years ago, and remember everything about her clearly in her mind.

For instance, she would recollect how Miss A would freeze to attention, standing to one side, whenever Miss Kimura passed her in the school corridor. Or there was her memory of Miss B, one of her favourite pupils, whom she had caught skylarking with a junior girl on the station platform. The girl had been so embarrassed that she had hidden herself in the Station Master's office! To her, such memories were full of poignant interest.

This was not, however, necessarily the reaction of the recipients of her letters, now mature women, who were thus abruptly brought face to face with memories of their youthful immaturity. Not all of them found Miss Kimura's recollections as welcome as she would have wished. These spectres of their past were suddenly produced, as if on film, before their very eyes, and most of the recipients found her letters distasteful or even shocking and did not vouchsafe replies.

A few, however, found the experience of value in helping them reflect on their personalities past and present. All of them had the same points in common; like their former teacher, they were living alone and were suffering from a feeling of spiritual oppression. For all of them, the prospects ahead seemed dark or non-existent, and only the past had any real meaning or comfort. Like her, they led secret lives apart from the real world.

When she had written exactly seven hundred such letters, the lot fell upon one Keiko Kawauchi (b. 1930). Yoneko Kimura had been her class teacher for the two years preceding graduation—and those were the two years immediately following Japan's wartime defeat, when society was in a turmoil and all the old values were being questioned.

Naturally, the former educational system was also being reviewed and revised at the same time.

The older teachers like Yoneko found some of the educational reforms that were being imposed on Japan by the Occupation Forces very hard to stomach. Until the textbooks could be reprinted, they had to go through them inking out passages reflecting militaristic or nationalistic thinking. Also, they had to reduce in number, and sometimes simplify in form, the Chinese characters they had been accustomed to teach in the past. The students soon sensed the uncertainty of their teachers who had for so long reigned inviolate from their raised dais, to whom the new word 'Liberty', with its effects overflowing into the classroom, began to assume repulsive connotations. Yoneko made just one attempt to recover her former dignity and state, and that had concerned Keiko Kawauchi. Most of the girls came to school in black cotton stockings. Some of the girls didn't have them, but most of the girls in the senior classes, the nubile ones, wore their uniform and black cotton stockings even though it was still a time of shortages and drab clothes in Japan. There was just one girl who was different—Keiko, who wore nylon stockings to school. Later on she had her imitators, but she was the first, and such clothes could only be obtained at great price through the black market. Seeing Keiko's shapely legs glittering in the smooth nylons, Yoneko's rage boiled up and overflowed. What angered her even more was the unladylike way in which Keiko sat with one thigh crossed over the other, as if to show off her legs and her stockings—such conduct in a young Japanese girl had been unthinkable before the coming of the Occupation Forces.

Looking back on the incident, Yoneko now wondered why she had worked herself up so much over a trivial detail, but at that time it had seemed a matter of great moment.

In fact, those nylon stockings were like the proverbial straw that broke the camel's back, and Yoneko's outburst of wrath merely reflected her deep dissatisfaction with the changes going on around her. Here was a threat, it seemed to her, to the whole structure of Japanese womanliness and morality, and it had to be faced head on. In stern tones, she rebuked the girl in front of the rest of the class, making it quite clear that nylon stockings were forbidden at school.

She had expected Keiko, after such public humiliation, to stay away from school for a day or two. In fact, she had herself begun to regret her over-reaction. But to the contrary, Keiko showed up at school the next day—still wearing nylon stockings. There were several other girls who, like Keiko, came from families which were prospering illicitly or indecently amidst the general ruin of the country, and these were the first to imitate her example. After a short while, all the girls in the class followed suit, until nylon stockings more or less became the fashion with school uniform. Yoneko came to realise that she no longer possessed the power to influence these adolescents of the postwar era, and accepted her defeat for want of any other course of action. The question was raised once at a teachers' conference, together with the new trend of schoolgirls growing their hair long, a thing formerly forbidden. All the teachers had to accept that their authority was diminished and that there was nothing to be done about such issues.

Keiko had graduated whilst the resentment of this incident still lay coiled in Yoneko's breast. Before her graduation, the school rustled with rumours that her elder sister had become a prostitute serving the needs of the US troops, but Keiko displayed no reaction whatever.

Yoneko's subsequent detailed knowledge of Keiko's career was based on the newspaper articles she had read at the time of the famous kidnapping incident seven years before. After leaving school, Keiko had gone to work in the Ginza PX, and within six months had married an American officer some fifteen years older than herself. At the time, Yoneko had felt that an evil fate seemed to dog Keiko, and that she was herself in part responsible. Subsequently, she had heard from one of the other girls that Keiko's venture into international marriage had failed, but she had no idea of her current whereabouts.

In her letter to Keiko, Yoneko made no reference to the kidnapping incident, but merely enquired after her present circumstances. She then touched lightly on the affair of the nylon stockings, and addressed the letter to Keiko's family home. She did not expect to get a reply—it would be another of those letters which were returned to her from time to time marked 'Gone away. Return to sender.'

But she received a reply very shortly afterwards. After her divorce, Keiko had gone back to her parents' home. She wrote about her school memories, and then went on as follows:

Teacher, you will certainly think my next request to be precipitate and stupid. I'm sure you'll think I haven't grown up at all, and am still just as self-centred as ever—please forgive me if you do.

You must have heard how, some years ago, my only son George was stolen from me by some unknown kidnapper. Seven years have passed, during which I have not enjoyed one day of peace in my heart. I keep trying to convince myself that I should give him up for lost, that it's best to forget him, but somehow I just can't. Deep inside me, I feel sure that George is still alive and well, somewhere, and that somewhere is in Japan.

Since returning to my family, they have constantly urged me to remarry, but I just can't with this heavy burden on my mind. I have spent all this time leaving no stone unturned in my search for my son.

When George was kidnapped, my former husband was the only person who spoke to the criminals. Looking back on it, I feel that if only I could have heard their voices, then perhaps I could have done something, but of course I just couldn't think straight at the time.

The kidnapping was all my fault. If only I had been more careful! At my husband's suggestion, I was having all my front teeth bridged, and so I was going to St Mark's Hospital every day. About a week before, George had begun to complain of toothache, so I made an appointment and took him with me that morning. They attended to him first, and then it was my turn. George didn't want to stay in the waiting room all that time, so I took him back to the car and left him there.

The dentist was particularly slow that day, fussing over whether he'd done a good job or not, and so it was a full thirty minutes before I got away. When I got back to the car, there was no sign of George. I asked around the neighbourhood, but no one had seen him.

Of course, he was then four years old, just the age when children like to do things by themselves, and he was never one to settle in any place for long. So I thought he had left the car of his own accord and was playing somewhere around the hospital.

Nonetheless, I phoned my husband right away, but unfortunately he was out of his office. Presuming that George would make his way back to the hospital, I reported his disappearance at the reception desk and then went back to the waiting room.

I waited till it got dark, but there was no sign of the boy. I tried to call my husband several times, but to no avail. In the end I drove back to our house in Denenchofu, and just as I got back my husband walked in.

As soon as he heard my story, my husband decided to go to the local police station. But just at that moment, those devils of kidnappers telephoned the house. If the call had been a few seconds later, I would have taken it and would have heard the kidnapper's voice. But as luck would have it, my husband was right by the phone when it rang. He picked up the receiver and listened, his face becoming grimmer all the time. Finally, he just said 'All right' and put the phone down. He then took my hands between his and earnestly bade me to do what he told me if we were ever to see George alive again. At the time, I went along with what he said, thinking it best under the circumstances. He said that if we were to save our son's life, I must promise not to contact the police, as he had done.

Well, as you know, the criminals broke their side of the promise. They betrayed us. We couldn't contact the police and get their help, but just had to wait for the one who phoned to contact us again—which he never did.

Even though it may be like crying over spilt milk, looking back now I really wish that I had insisted on calling the police right away. At the time, I didn't want to go against my husband for fear of hurting him, but within a year of George's disappearance our marital life came to an end anyway. We divorced, and the alimony he agreed to pay me left me with no financial worries, so that I was able to devote myself to searching for George. I went up and down the length and breadth of Japan, visiting every Christian orphanage and school where mixed-blood children are to be found, but all to no avail.

Those about me pointed out that a half-caste child could not just get lost in the crowd like a pure-blooded Japanese, and that there was no point in aimlessly searching without even the basis of a rumour to go on. I could not but accept the logic of their view, but nonetheless it was unacceptable to me and I carried on just the same.

In addition, the police were doing their best to find George, but without success.

I had felt sure that sometime, somehow or other, I would hear about George. But as the days and months and years passed with no tidings whatever, I began to give up hope and even resign myself to the prospect of never hearing from him again.

And then, just recently, two things happened that rekindled my hopes. First of all, I still make it my habit to pass by my old house in Denenchofu at least once a day, and walk about the neighbourhood in the faint hope that George might just remember his past and turn up in the area. Well, I was in that vicinity the other day when a young man who wore the uniform of one of our best universities called out to me across the street.

I took it he was mistaking me for someone else until he made it clear that he recognised me as George's mother. Then

I remembered him. He was Fumio Kurokawa, the son of our old daily maid. Although he was some four years older than George, he used to come and play with him from time to time.

He expressed his sympathy to me concerning George, and then told me how he happened to be in the neighbourhood:

'It's ages since I've been round here, but we've been having our annual classmates' reunion at my primary school. Everything seems to have changed since our day! Big shiny new concrete buildings, and half the teachers are new. However, they'd got out some of our old work—pictures we'd painted, test papers, essays and so forth. And, do you know what, one of my early compositions was on display—"My little foreign friend" it was called, and it was all about George! So it's really rather appropriate that I should bump into you again after all these years!'

He went on to describe what he'd written, and one thing really made me think. You see, he'd described in detail how I used to go to the dentist every morning at that time, and how I used to take George with me. There was our daily life being set down in a Japanese child's essay, detail by detail, and all without our knowing.

Furthermore, the essay subject was specially set for him by his teacher, a Miss Chikako Ueda, who no longer teaches there.

Well, since then, I've been thinking more and more about young Kurokawa's essay. And the more I think about it, the more I feel convinced that there is some link between that essay and George's disappearance. It's as if, after all these years, I've suddenly found the traces of a footprint of my vanished child.

I fully realise that this is just a wild fancy, and I promise you I am trying to resign myself to the inevitable. But a drowning man will clutch at any straw, and the fact that you wrote to me on the same day seems possibly to be more than a mere coincidence.

I don't mean just the letter itself, although it aroused sweet memories in my heart to receive a letter from my old teacher. When I saw your address on the back of the envelope, I suddenly realised that you are living in the same apartment block as the teacher who set Fumio Kurokawa to write an essay on his little foreign friend all those years ago. I am not a religious person, but at that moment I began to tremble all over—it seemed as if, at last, Divine Providence was beginning to take a hand in my affairs.

After seven years of darkness, I think I can at last see a little ray of light ahead.

Of course, I wouldn't dream of suggesting that Miss Chikako Ueda was directly involved in the kidnapping. I just wonder if she remembers letting anyone else see that essay at that time. So if you happen to speak to her at any time, I wonder if you could raise the subject delicately and see what you can find out.

I beg you to excuse the self-centredness of a woman who has lost her only child and, if it is not too much trouble, to do what you can to help me.

Yours sincerely,
Keiko Kawauchi

It would not be going too far to say that this letter altered the whole course of the rest of Yoneko Kimura's life. She had written several hundred rather meaningless letters to her former pupils just to pass the time; now at last one of them was to bear dramatic fruit.

Although they lived in the same building, they were on different floors, so Yoneko knew very little about Chikako Ueda. She had passed her in the hallway a few times, that was all.

She spent the next week collecting information on her quarry, discreetly questioning her neighbours and the receptionists. The following facts emerged:

1. She had quit her job as a primary school teacher six years previously, giving out that she was getting married.

2. But there had been no sign of a suitor, let alone a marriage, and she had subsequently spent most of her time locked in her room alone.

3. She had for the last few years begun to act and speak in a rather strange way, casting doubts on her mental stability.

All of which being so, Yoneko realised that no purpose would be served by approaching Chikako direct. Not that this would have been easy, as Chikako's whole course of behaviour and way of life seemed to be contrived in order to avoid meeting or talking with anyone. It did indeed seem as if she had something to hide.

Yoneko decided to keep Chikako under close observation for a time before proceeding further. She wrote back to Keiko, telling her of what she had learned and asking her former pupil to leave the matter entirely in her hands. She said that she would share with her the grief and pain that Keiko had suffered. This was all very well, but of course she had absolutely no idea of what she might be called upon to do when the time came. For the time being, all she could do was to try and get a peep inside Chikako's room.

She continued her practice of writing one letter a day to her former students, but with less enthusiasm than before. On her way out to post them every morning, she would glance at the master key and secretly envy the receptionist within whose power it lay to enter every room in the block.

It was essential that she should get her hands on that key.

A few days later, Yoneko was to be found at the bottom of the stairway, peering down through the receptionist's hatch. Miss Tojo was on duty; as usual, she was sitting with her head lowered as if concentrating on some book or document on the desk. But more to the point, the master key, readily identifiable from its red ribbon and large wooden tag, was also on the desk. This was in accordance with a resolution passed by the residents' association shortly after the Suwa Yatabe incident.

Yoneko went up to the receptionist's window. 'I'm sorry to disturb you, but could I just have a look at the fourth-floor gas bills for last month?' she asked. (She had just taken up a three-month spell of duty as committee member for the fourth floor.)

'Miss Suzuki is complaining that her bill was too high last month. She says her meter must have been misread. She's not the kind to take no for an answer, so if you don't mind…' she explained.

'No trouble at all. After all, it's my job—I'll certainly go and have a look.' Miss Tojo got up and went to the back of the room and began to rummage in the filing cabinet. The master key lay within reach of Yoneko's hand. Could she make the switch now, she wondered. She stretched her hand through the window.'

Two days earlier, she had been listening outside Chikako's door on the fifth floor when Miss Tojo had suddenly appeared. As Chikako's room was second from the far end of the corridor, Yoneko had nowhere to hide. She started to try and cover up her unwarranted presence there by asking Miss Tojo who was the fifth-floor committee representative, but she need not have worried. As luck would have it, Miss Tojo was holding the master key and in search of a witness before she used it. The rule was that the witness should either be from a neighbouring room or a committee member. So, far from being curious as to why Yoneko was on the fifth floor, she was delighted to find her there. It so happened that Miss Haru Santo, who occupied the room next to Chikako's, had telephoned to say that she had left her electric stove on. They let themselves in, and indeed found the stove on and the kettle boiled nearly dry.

'It's not particularly the fire risk that worried her—after all, there's not much danger of that. No, it was the fear of incurring a high electricity bill that got her. She pretends to earn her living teaching Japanese to foreigners, but we know better than that, don't we!' Miss Tojo switched the stove off as she spoke.

Yoneko understood the implications of her last remark. Some while back, one of the other residents had visited one of the main Tokyo cinemas and, going to the toilet, had been surprised to find that the cleaner there bore a striking resemblance to Miss Santo. But the cleaner had made good her escape before any words could be exchanged.

110

Yoneko knew little more about Miss Santo apart from the fact that she had snow-white hair and was a fervent adherent of a new spiritualist sect called the '*Sanreikyo*'.* Perhaps her unusually white hair owed something to her fanaticism; at all events, she was a slightly creepy little old woman.

There was a small altar by the black curtain festooned with weird talismans; on top of it, there was a religious offering of rice wine. The whole room reeked of incense. All in all, it fully resembled what one would imagine the apartment of a devotee of a new religion to be like, and the fact that such a mundane reason as an electric stove had led her there caused Yoneko to find her surroundings even more strange.

'But I'm glad people phone me without embarrassment when such things occur,' said Miss Tojo, as she locked the door. 'Since that fire in Miss Ishiyama's room, it's just as well to take full precautions.'

'Yes—and it's just as well you have a master key. What a convenient thing that is! You can get into anyone's room...' Yoneko replied vacuously, but the power of the master key had begun to obsess her.

'Not just convenient; it's a disaster if it gets mislaid. Just think of that recent incident where we found it still in the lock on the inside of Miss Yatabe's room! We still haven't got to the bottom of that one, but what a peculiar set of circumstances that was! We took every care, but it still vanished. You know, the builders of this place were ahead of their time. Just think how long it would take if there were no master key, and if we had to search through

* Literally 'Three spirit faith.'

111

a hundred and fifty keys every time there was a problem like this! It showed real imagination to make one key to fit all the locks. Look, I'll show you how it differs from all the other keys—do you see this groove here, at the tip?'

And she went prattling on about how this building had been the first in Japan to employ such a master key. And how essential a thing this had been at the time for an apartment block reserved solely for the use of unmarried young women.

Yoneko Kimura spent that evening considering how she could get her hands on that master key, which could solve her problem. Eventually she came up with a plan.

Since the key spent the daytime under the nose of the receptionist, and the nights in a locker, the only apparent way to get hold of it was to break into the office at night and steal it from the locker. But this would involve forcing two locks, which was beyond her power. So if it had to be stolen by daytime, one would have to remove it by force, which she also had to rule out. There remained the possibility of explaining the whole thing frankly to the receptionist and asking for the loan of the key. Nonetheless, however correct her motivation, the receptionist would almost certainly abide by the rules and refer the matter to the residents' committee for a decision. The request would almost certainly be rejected on the grounds of protection of privacy.

And so there was only one way left—sleight of hand. When the master key had been used to enter Miss Santo's room, Yoneko had for the first time got a close look at it. Apart from a slight difference of patina, it hardly seemed any different from all the individual keys, including her own, used about the building. What distinguished it from the others was the wooden tag tied to it with a red ribbon.

Yoneko got out her own key and looked at it. It seemed to differ in no noticeable way from the master key. If it had a red ribbon and a wooden tag, it would look just like the master key. The red ribbon would present no problem, but forging the wooden tag and the writing on it might prove more hard. It would take some time to age a new piece of wood with sweat and grime. But then she noticed that the keys to the lavatory broom cupboards had an identical wooden tag—and this key was always left in the door of the cupboard where anyone could get at it! So she quietly removed the tag and the ribbon of the second-floor lavatory cupboard one day and soiled the ribbon until it looked just like that on the master key. She then tied the tag to her own room key.

Her plan was somehow to distract the receptionist's attention and switch the master key with her own key on the lavatory tag, with the writing face down. If the exchange was not noticed right away by the receptionist, she should be able to effect her purpose. For when the switch finally came to light, even if she was accused of it she could deny all knowledge of the matter. What mattered was to get hold of the key and investigate Chikako Ueda's room; once that was accomplished, she could pretend that her room key had been swapped at some stage without her knowledge, probably by the very person who had stolen the master key before.

And now that key lay within her reach. She stealthily moved her hand towards it; suddenly, without warning, Miss Tojo turned around.

'Is it in that drawer, do you think?' said Yoneko, lifting her hand quickly off the desk and pointing it at the cabinet behind Miss Tojo. Her voice faltered under the stress.

'The receipts should be in the same drawer as the daily reports, but there are so many documents in there…' Miss Tojo peered confusedly at the open drawer.

'Maybe I could help?'

'Oh, please do. Please come in.'

That was just the reply Yoneko was hoping for. Now she could get behind the counter, which would considerably increase her chance of making the exchange. She went through the office door for the very first time in her life; the room, she noticed, was very tidy. A book lay opened face down on the swivel chair behind the desk; Miss Tojo had indeed been reading whilst pretending to be busily engaged in her work. Yoneko herself loved reading, and felt a sudden affinity for Miss Tojo. She tried to catch a glance of the book's title, but it was concealed behind a plain brown wrapper.

'It's certainly somewhere in this drawer.' Just at that moment, the office phone rang.

'I'll just take that call while you have a look.' Miss Tojo pulled out the drawer and carried it bodily to the office desk and put it down just by the master key. She then went to answer the phone, leaving Yoneko to leaf through the piles of receipts. She soon came upon the receipt she was seeking, but pretended not to have found it.

'Hold on a moment please,' said Miss Tojo to the caller. 'I'll just go and check—you did say Miss Munekata on the second floor, didn't you?'

Miss Tojo put down the receiver and, pausing only to glance for a second at the book, the master key and the files, hurried out of the office. What a heaven-sent chance, thought Yoneko, as she fished into her blouse pocket and brought out the tag with her own room key on it. She placed it beside the master key and compared the two carefully. The ribbon was a little fresher-looking, but the keys themselves appeared without close examination to be identical. It didn't seem as if the exchange would be noticed.

She was just about to slip the genuine master key into her pocket when it suddenly occurred to her that she might switch the wooden labels. She had no idea if she had time to undo the ribbons and retie them, but if she could succeed in doing so, it would be quite some time before the exchange would be detected.

She decided to take the risk, and set to work on the ribbon of the real master key. The knot was a little tight, but by using her fingernails she soon had it undone. So far, so good; her hands were hardly even trembling.

But the knot she had tied on her own room key a day or two before was a different matter. She kept counselling herself not to panic, but it seemed as if the knot could not be undone. Just as she was about to give up and leave the key on the desk as she had originally planned, the knot loosened, and so she decided to carry on after all. She began to attach the tag to her own room key.

She heard footsteps on the stairs before she was half done; it was bound to be Miss Tojo making her way back. She slipped the key and tag into the drawer and pretended to be riffling through the receipts. Her hands began to shake, but after two or more attempts she managed to thread the ribbon through the head of the key.

The footsteps stopped outside the door, which then opened, and Miss Tojo came back in. Yoneko felt she could sense the receptionist's gaze, even though her back was turned to her. She still had to fasten the ribbon; if she could quickly thread it through the key once more, that would do. She held the receipts in her right hand whilst her left hand worked on the key lying in the drawer. Using her thumb and index finger, she got the ribbon through the hole. One knot more, and it could not possibly work loose. Miss Tojo went to the telephone receiver just by Yoneko.

'Hullo! Miss Munekata is a little busy and so cannot take your call. I'm sorry, but she says she'll call you back.'

She turned to Yoneko. '"Inconvenient", she says. Everything's always inconvenient to Miss Munekata. I suppose she doesn't worry about other people's convenience.'

She was obviously annoyed at being put out for nothing. 'Ah! I've found it at last,' said Yoneko. 'I'll just take the drawer back over there.'

She picked the drawer up, and then let it fall with a crash to the ground. It landed face down, and all the receipts and documents were scattered over the floor. Miss Tojo got on her knees and began to pick them up again. Under cover of this distraction, Yoneko was able to put the key on the desk.

'Oh! I'm so sorry! How silly of me!' Whilst saying this, Yoneko picked up the book which was lying face down on the chair and glanced at the title. *Words from the Spirit World*—it meant nothing to her.

Miss Tojo turned round and saw what Yoneko was doing. Her features clouded with suspicion, and she quickly glanced over to where the master key, or, rather, its substitute, was lying on the desk.

Yoneko had no idea what the receptionist must be thinking. She felt embarrassed, and after making a few hasty apologies, withdrew without bothering to take that so important gas bill with her.

It was some days later, when Miss Munekata gassed herself, that the master key was discovered to have been switched. As this was just the latest such event, the receptionists (neither wishing to take any blame) professed total ignorance of how it had come about. Such, at least, was Yoneko's interpretation of their silence.

About a week after Yoneko Kimura took the master key, a meeting of the residents' committee was called. The loss of the key was high on the agenda.

During those seven days, Yoneko had been awaiting her chance to get into Chikako Ueda's room but, just as normal, Chikako never seemed to go out at all. It appeared that the one exception to this rule was her weekly expedition to the grocer's, where she would stock up with tinned foods and other durables. How she passed the remainder of her time alone in her room remained a mystery.

It had seemed unlikely that there would be any call for the master key to be used in that short period and so its loss would not have been discovered but for the accident on the second floor. A strong smell of gas was detected outside Miss Munekata's room, and in the ensuing confusion the theft became known. Now Yoneko could only wait and let matters take their own course.

It appeared that Miss Munekata had gone to sleep

leaving the gas stove on, and somehow the flame had been extinguished. One of her neighbours had got up to go to the toilet in the middle of the night, and had noticed the smell of gas exuding from the fanlight window above Toyoko Munekata's room. It was fortunate that the discovery was made so early, thus avoiding a fatal accident.

Miss Kimura was aroused from her bed in the front office and, rubbing the sleep from her eyes, tried repeatedly to open Miss Munekata's door with the master key. Needless to say, it did not work, but it took some time for Miss Kimura to realise that this was not due to some failure on her own part, and she spent several minutes reinserting the key in the lock and rattling it to and fro. At last she gave up, and the fire brigade was called. An ambulance with two acrobatic firemen on board arrived in a twinkling; one of them climbed onto a chair and squirmed through the fanlight until he could reach and remove the key from the lock inside. They got into Toyoko Munekata's room and removed her unconscious body into the open air. She was still breathing faintly and so her life was saved.

If that had been all there was to it, there need have been no further repercussions. However, when they opened the window to air the room, a strong breeze blew in, disturbing the papers on the desk and eventually scattering them all over the place.

The residents had heard how precious the manuscript was, and so several of them entered the room and hastily retrieved the scattered papers. As they did so, they could not help noticing the peculiar mathematical formulae and symbols—triangles, circles, and childish doodles, and even obscene phrases—which made up the text. Rumours swiftly spread around the apartment block, to the effect that Toyoko's great work was no more than a sham, and that she was touched in the head.

When Yoneko heard this, she was horrified to think that her theft of the master key had nearly brought about the death of a fellow resident. Furthermore, her action had indirectly led to Toyoko Munekata becoming a laughing stock, so that her continued occupancy of the apartment block was imperilled. She felt that Toyoko's daily labours on the manuscripts of her dead husband were similar in many ways to her own daily letters to her former pupils. And so she could not bring herself to join the chorus of scorn directed towards Toyoko.

'Just think of it,' said her fellow committee member. 'All circles and triangles and crosses.' She was a school teacher, and had long been resentful of Toyoko's superior manner. 'She told us that unlike us she was engaged on a real work of scholarship! Well, that wind certainly showed her up.'

'But we can't imagine that her late husband's research consisted only of such things,' interrupted Yoneko, springing to Toyoko's defence. 'I can't pretend to be an authority on higher mathematics, but I have heard that once you get to the philosophical level things are not as simple as they appear. I once read somewhere that to a mathematician a circle, or a wheel, say, is not perfectly round at all but is made up of an infinite number of angles.' She was echoing the thesis she had heard from an enthusiastic young mathematician years ago in the school common room.

'That's true,' agreed the first-floor representative, who worked in a museum. 'My late husband was a professor of classical Greek. He used to write down all sorts of words and compose vocabularies in those funny letters; it looked more like a childish game than the work of a grown man.'

The committee was assembled for a meeting in the drawing room on the first floor. This room was rarely used and was in consequence dusty and had a mouldy smell. They sat around a large table, on top of which was placed a kettle, teacups and small cakes wrapped in cellophane.

The meeting had been called for six. It was now ten past, but the chairman had not yet arrived. She was a highly skilled and very experienced shorthand secretary who worked at the local council, taking the minutes, and was one of the most highly paid residents in the building. She was very public-spirited, and had served as chairman of the residents' representative committee without a break for the last five years. The system was that one representative was elected for each floor for a full term of one year, and a further representative was elected for a term of three months. The chairman was also specially elected once a year, making a total of eleven members on the committee. However, at most meetings four or five members would be absent on other business, so the average attendance was about five or six plus the chairman.

The agenda for this specially called meeting consisted of two items, one of them being the perennial problem of cat messes. But the second topic was of much greater interest, and so there was an unusually high attendance, only two of the members being unable to come.

The item of particular concern was the planned move-ment of the whole building, which had been announced some six months before. Work was due to begin in just one more week.

The door swung open with a crash and a stout female figure came in cautiously as if expecting to find the space too narrow to squeeze through. It was the chairman, Miss Yoko Tanikawa; she was wearing a jacket of masculine cut and had a briefcase under her arm.

'Sorry to keep you waiting! I had to clarify a few last-minute points about the move, which is on the agenda.'

She sat down at the head of the table and opened her case, producing various documents which she placed in orderly piles on the table.

'Well, as you all know, they'll get started on the move from next week. However, there are just one or two problems which need to be kept in mind. For instance, there's the noise, which will be pretty troublesome. Then there'll be all the dust—they're digging out all the foundations, you see. However, taking the broad view, let us not forget that this is being done for the public good. It's all part of the overall city plan for road-widening, and it is incumbent on all of us to cooperate and to put up with the inconvenience. However, there are limits—just because it is necessary to move the building does not in my view mean that we have to put up with workmen wandering in and out and disturbing our privacy. I would remind you all of how insecure we feel now that the master key has once more vanished. These apartments were founded with the intention of preserving the modesty and so enhancing the status of working women. That one little key was the guarantor of these aims, but in the wrong hands it becomes a threat. In such circumstances, locked doors lose their meaning!'

She sighed deeply, and then went on to say that the loss of the master key would be discussed in greater detail

121

later on in the meeting. Before that, it would be necessary to determine what conditions should be applied to the construction workers during the course of the work. When she had finished talking, she passed the cakes and tea around the table.

'Well, surely if it's to do with the construction, we will just have to put up with people coming in and out, won't we?' The speaker was the representative of the third floor, who had recently received a commendation for her long services at the tourist company where she worked.

'I couldn't disagree more! That way, we'll have every Tom, Dick and Harry coming and going as they please. If you ask me, everything's getting too lax, and we should take a firm stand somewhere, and the sooner the better. Nowadays, we're too soft on a lot of things, from the upbringing of the young to such matters as letting people keep cats, which leave insanitary droppings all over the corridors. That's one thing I don't intend to put up with any more round here. And if that wasn't enough, we now have a peculiar man being allowed to come and go at will on the pretext that he is a missionary for one of these new-fangled religions!'

This angry outburst came from the full representative of the second floor, who had lately been promoted to section chief, the first woman in the history of her company to achieve such a rank. The alternate member for the first floor, Tomiko Iyoda, who was sitting on Yoneko Kimura's right, bridled visibly during this speech and sprang to her feet when it was over. Not only was it her cat to which reference had been made, but she was also the recruiting member for the Three Spirit Faith which had been obliquely criticised.

'Take that back at once! How dare you refer to His Reverence in that way—a peculiar man indeed! And as if that wasn't enough, you attack me through my little cat as well! I'll have you know that I always clear up any mess he makes.' She then lowered her voice a key and went on: 'I will ignore your lies about my cat, but let me warn you that divine retribution invariably awaits those who slander His Reverence!' She wanted to go on, but her neighbour, the full representative for the first floor, tugged her by the sleeve. Tomiko Iyoda was thus forced to sit down, but for a while she continued to glare angrily at her opponent, mouthing voiceless imprecations the while.

Miss Tanikawa, the chairman, behaved as if nothing had happened, calling on the next speaker, the member of the fifth floor, who was an employee of the local welfare office.

'While the move is being effected, it will be necessary to disconnect such public utilities as the gas, the electricity and the water. Also, the whole programme will only take a relatively short time. I therefore think it both pointless and impossible absolutely to forbid the workmen to come and go as necessary. In any case, there are no grounds for classifying all the workmen as criminals or in any other way bad. If, when the time comes, anyone is worried they can go straight to the ladies at the reception desk and report any suspicious circumstances.'

'That's all very well,' said someone else, 'but you know what men are like. Before you know what's happening, they'll be forcing their way into our rooms asking for a cup of tea or something!'

After some further debate, it seemed to be the general consensus that the workmen should be trusted and not all regarded as potential thieves or worse. However, each member of the committee would take it in turn to patrol the building during the period of the work. Miss Tanikawa summed up with a humorous suggestion. 'We'll have an armband made with "Security Patrol" in big bright letters. It will serve as a kind of PR, and it mightn't be a bad idea if the duty member carries a night-stick as well.'

The harmonious atmosphere thus created was soon destroyed by the member for the second floor, who returned to her earlier topic.

'Madam Chair. I must raise an emergency item which is not on the agenda. I refer of course to the menace posed by those who have recently been pestering and pressurising our fellow residents with their campaign on behalf of a new religion. As Madam Chair so rightly remarked earlier, the prime objective of these apartments is to protect the privacy of the individual residents. I am absolutely opposed to those who force their way into other people's rooms, like foot-in-the-door salesmen, in the name of religion. I want it stopped; several of my constituents on the second floor have already complained to me about it. I propose that the most stringent measures be taken to stamp out this practice.'

'And who do you think you are to make such suggestions! I'll have you know that religious freedom is protected under the constitution. The Three Spirit Faith never pressures anyone. Who are they who complain of being pestered? Let's have their names, one by one!'

'I don't see why I should give you all their names. But as an example, we had the recent unfortunate incident when Miss Munekata nearly lost her life through gas poisoning.

Now the word is going around that this was a so-called divine retribution visited on her for refusing to join your sect.'

'She was punished by Heaven for slandering His Reverence. She came to the last public meeting and dared to confute His Reverence point by point on his exposition. She made him seem foolish in the eyes of the unbelievers, so His Reverence prophesied at that very time that ill would befall those who close their hearts to the True Teaching. What has occurred is no more than the fulfilment of his prophecy.'

'Oh really—how very interesting. You say that the prophecy was followed by heavenly punishment, but it looks to me as if some mortal was responsible for this so-called divine retribution! It's the first I've heard of a gas stove falling over and the fire going out. I don't see how that could happen naturally—if you ask me, there was more to it than met the eye. Could it not be that someone switched off the gas at the stop-cock outside the room and then turned it on again?'

This was certainly possible, for as the member for the second floor had remarked, every apartment had its own separate gas meter and stop-cock outside, and it would be a simple matter for someone malicious to do as she had suggested. Indeed, Yoneko had entertained the same suspicion from the moment she had first heard of the incident. She wondered what the representative of the Three Spirit Faith would have to say to this insinuation.

The alternate member from the first floor sprang to her feet at once, but was for a few seconds too dumbfounded to reply. After spluttering with anger for a while, she began:

'What possible evidence have you for such allegations? Don't you know that the fire brigade made a thorough investigation and concluded that the kettle boiled over and put out the flame? Are you now implying that the Three Spirit Faith planned the whole thing? If so, I can promise you a writ for slander in no time at all!'

As she worked herself up into a passion, the speaker's lips became flecked with foam, and a small globule of spittle landed on the table just in front of Yoneko.

The member for the second floor refused to admit defeat. 'You don't really mean to suggest that the gas was on so low that a little water from the kettle could put it out? If so, how could the kettle boil over?'

The atmosphere of the meeting was poisoned by further such debate, after which a vote was called on whether or not religious proselytising would be permitted in the building. After everyone had had their say, it appeared that the member for the second floor had four votes, as against two for the representative of the Three Spirit Faith, with one probable abstainer, and so Yoneko Kimura's vote looked like being decisive. If she supported the motion, it would achieve an absolute majority and be passed, but if she opposed it the proposal would be shelved.

She gazed at the voting slip which lay before her, trying to make up her mind what to do. The regular members had cast their votes and folded the papers with practised speed. Just as she was about to set her pen to the paper, she became aware of the intent gaze of the woman from the Three Spirit Faith, who was staring at her hands as if seeking to hypnotise her. And so it was, perhaps, that she cast a negative vote causing the resolution to fail.

It was already past eight pm, but before they could bring the meeting to a close it was necessary to discuss the latest incident involving the master key. Chairman Tanikawa gazed around the table and addressed the group.

'I think you will all have shared my disgust at learning that the master key disappeared under the very noses of the receptionists. It was bad enough when it happened the first time—you will all know of the incident last month when it was used to gain entry into Miss Yatabe's room. It's not good enough for the receptionists merely to express astonishment—I would like to see them at least display concern that such a thing can happen. One would expect a greater show of responsibility, would one not? But so soon after the first incident had brought home to us all the importance of the master key, it vanished again. I ask you, ladies, what next? How could they have failed to notice that the key had been switched? All the excuse they could find was to say that some supernatural agency was at work! Disgraceful, I call it, quite disgraceful!

'However, there's no point in shutting the stable door after the horse has gone. Let us rather resolve to identify and weed out the mischief-maker in our midst. I would like the cooperation of each one of you in finding out where the master key has gone.'

She held up something for everyone to see. 'This is the key which was exchanged for the master key. If you examine it closely, you will see it is exactly like a typical apartment key from this building. I suggest that we concentrate on identifying the owner—how about it?'

'Well, it certainly looks like an apartment key, but what do you suggest we do?' asked one of the committee.

'We could just ask every person in the building to show us her key. However, a large number of people would be involved, and the whole thing would smack of a police investigation, which would not be nice. So I propose instead that we take it in turns to try this key in every door until we find which lock it fits. When we find out who it belongs to, we'll ask her for a satisfactory explanation.'

Yoneko sat frozen in her seat. She listened in a daze to the even voice of the representative of the fifth floor as she asked the next question. 'That's all very well, but surely it is likely to fit several doors?'

This left Miss Tanikawa nonplussed for a moment or two.

'Yes, well, um… Yes, maybe. Anyway, let's just try it and see. Obviously, if we can think of a better method, we'll switch to that when the time comes.'

And the chairman's proposal was passed unanimously.

'Well, let's get started first thing tomorrow. Let's start on the top floor and work our way down in order. Representatives are to be responsible for their own floors. Let's try and avoid attracting attention to what we're doing—try each door only after checking that the occupant is out. It could be embarrassing otherwise.'

'Most people are out at work in the daytime, but what shall we say to those who aren't?'

'In that case, you'll just have to play innocent. Say something like "Isn't this your key?" and put it in the lock to see. Well, that will do for today—same time and place next week.'

Miss Tanikawa brought the meeting to a close as quickly as possible before anyone else could protract the proceedings with further discussion.

As Yoneko filed out of the room, she found the third-floor representative, the delegate for the Three Spirit Faith, awaiting her in the corridor. That lady approached her and addressed her in an unpleasant tone of voice.

'The spirit of His Reverence descended upon you, and was within you, forcing you even against your own will to vote on our side.'

And then she went on to urge Yoneko to attend at least one of the sect's meetings to see for herself the power of which the elder was possessed.

'He will ease all your sufferings, however great they may be. Of course, he can heal illnesses or discover lost objects if you ask him to. At present, he is fixing his mind on something that Miss Yatabe on the first floor has mislaid. Next week, he will hold a special prayer session, and I've no doubt he'll reveal where it is then. Anyway, won't you just join us once?'

Yoneko turned her away with a non-committal reply and made her way back to her room. She had more to think of than religious meetings; however interesting they might seem. She was far more concerned about the resolution at the meeting which could lead to the discovery of her possession of the master key.

If everything proceeded according to schedule, the search would reach the fourth floor in two days' time. On which day a senior floor representative, Taeko Nakagawa, would return from a visit to the country. And when she did, Yoneko would have to accompany her from room to room, trying the key in every door until it became clear that it was *her* lock in which it fitted, making public her guilt.

Now she deeply regretted the light-hearted attitude which had led her to switch the master key for her own. Why had she been so short-sighted? Looking back on her own stupidity, she could not think what had come over her to act as she had.

PART SEVEN

The Three Spirit Faith

After supper, the corridors echoed for a while with the sound of people walking up and down, the clatter of dishes and the splash of running water in the communal wash-place. Then silence fell upon the building, to occupy it, usually, for the rest of the night.

Sometimes, one would hear the sound of a radio or the muffled tones of someone practising on the trumpet. But these noises also subsided after a little while, until it became so quiet that one could hear the switches, one by one, being turned off for the night.

It was at about eight o'clock two evenings after the committee meeting. A shadowy figure crept stealthily towards Yoneko's door, moving secretively as if not wishing to be discovered.

Yoneko was in her room, composing her third letter to her former pupil, Keiko Kawauchi. She pored over the paper on her desk, writing carefully in the dim light of her standard lamp.

Having explained how she had purloined the master key in order to get into Chikako Ueda's room, she went on to describe that day's events.

This afternoon, our floor was searched. There were three of us involved—myself, Miss Nakagawa and Miss Tamura from the front desk. We went from door to door, trying it in every lock. Can you imagine your teacher's feelings, Keiko, as we got closer to my room? I still had no idea of what I would say or do when the truth came out. I suppose I'd have just tried to feign as much astonishment as everyone else when the door swung open. But fortunately things turned out better than that.

You see, we were taking it in turns to try the key, and the lot fell to me for my section of the corridor. Looking as innocent as I could, I stood in front of my own door and tried to turn the key. I must admit I felt pretty scared, but I put on a good act and, as you can imagine, somehow, however hard I tried, I could not make that key turn! Of course, I was in a cold sweat all the time! Well…

At that moment, Yoneko heard a stealthy knock on her door.
  'Who is it?'
There was no reply. Yoneko opened the door a little and peeped out into the dark passage. She could just make out a dim figure standing in the gloom. A voice as chilly and slight as the draught which was flowing into the room whispered:
  'Miss Kimura! His Reverence's prayer meeting and revelation of lost things will take place at eight-thirty. He has given exceptional permission for you to attend the seance, so I trust you will not let us down, will you? Please come to Miss Iyoda's room on the first floor at eight-thirty sharp.'
And without waiting for a reply, the ghost-like figure slipped away into the shadows.
The girl who disappeared thus without Yoneko getting a proper look at her was indeed a strange figure. Her child-like body was topped by an adult head; had she but known it, Yoneko's visitor was none other than the woman nicknamed 'Thumbelina the Vestal'.

Thumbelina reached a pool of light on the landing, and there silently held up a black notebook. She opened it and placed a mark against the name 'Yoneko Kimura' written there in large characters.

Her name did not belie her, for in addition to her petite stature she was, like her namesake, exquisitely beautiful. She was young, and her long black hair shone with camellia oil. It hung in a heavy mass, swinging elegantly as she moved. Perhaps she had applied white makeup to her face and neck in the old-fashioned way; in any case, her skin was unnaturally and beautifully pallid. She was dressed like a priestess from a Shinto shrine, in the traditional white coat and loose red trousers.

Having closed the notebook, she looked at the watch on her wrist. Just about eight! There was something touchingly incongruous about a watch on so tiny and childish a wrist.

She made her way up to the fifth floor and walked straight into the end room as if she was quite accustomed to doing so without knocking. This room belonged to one Haru Santo, and was next to that of Chikako Ueda.

Haru Santo was kneeling in front of her personal shrine. Apart from the candles flickering in its recesses, the room was pitch dark. Her white hair shone eerily in the gloom. The candles seemed to light up every strand as if it was burnished silver wire, making it seem artificial, rather than a natural growth.

Thumbelina the Vestal slipped in beside Haru Santo and prostrated herself thrice before the altar. Then she swivelled around on her knees, placing her beautiful face next to the old woman's ear, and whispered something for several minutes.

When she left Haru Santo's room twenty minutes later, it was almost time for the seance to begin. She hurriedly made her way down to the first floor.

That gave Yoneko Kimura her first chance of getting a look at her. Having finished her letter to Keiko Kawauchi, she had been in two minds as to whether to attend the seance or not, but had nevertheless gone downstairs. She had expected to find Miss Tojo at the front desk, but Miss Tamura was on duty. Apparently Miss Tojo had had to go out at short notice, and so had asked her colleague to sit in for her.

'Well, that key doesn't fit any of the doors on the fourth or fifth floors. So what's the betting we'll find the culprit tomorrow on the third floor?'

Listening to Miss Tamura's friendly gossip, Yoneko noticed Thumbelina coming down the staircase. It gave her such a start that she could not restrain a gasp. There was something truly weird about the little priestess. Yoneko gave up all thought of attending the seance, and rushed back up the stairs towards her room. But on the landing she bumped into Tomiko Iyoda, a seller of lottery tickets, in whose room the meeting was about to be held. She was leading a small group downstairs.

'Well, well, Miss Kimura, how nice to see you! Come on down with us. The vestal spoke to you, I think? Good! Well, we're just about to start.'

And so it came about that Yoneko Kimura attended a seance of the Three Spirit Faith.

All sorts of shoes and sandals were neatly arranged in the little lobby of Miss Iyoda's room, suggesting the variety and number of their owners crowded inside.

'Well, I apologise for the state everything is in, but please come inside.'

Tomiko Iyoda, speaking in sweet tones, drew Yoneko and her companions in after her.

There were some six people already sitting on the floor of the tiny room, surrounding a middle-aged man in a double-breasted suit. He had the look of a priest about him, and seemed to be delivering a sermon, which he broke off on the entry of Yoneko and the others.

'I'm so sorry we kept Your Reverence waiting,' said Miss Iyoda. She waddled over to the corner and, bending her fat body with evident signs of discomfort, picked up a pile of cushions and handed them around for the new arrivals to sit on. She then took her place next to the priest.

Yoneko sat next to the door, and, peering over the shoulder of the elderly woman in front of her, took in the scene. Miss Iyoda was plainly briefing the priest on the new arrivals; this was obvious, even though she spoke in a low voice. The priest seemed to be a man in his fifties. His angular face was framed by black hair glued down with pomade. He had bright red cheeks, and this sign of cheerful vigour was reinforced by the gusty laughs with which he punctuated his discourse, but once he caught your eye… Yoneko was forced to gaze downwards, so overcome was she by his sharp and questing gaze. It was as if he could read right into the hidden depths of her mind.

Amongst those present, there were some Yoneko knew by sight, but not one with whom she had ever exchanged a word. There were even some present who did not live in the building. They were all in their forties or fifties, and without exception their faces were those of people defeated by life.

'Your Reverence, all is now ready. Pray begin when you wish.'

The low vibrant voice in which this remark was delivered seemed to echo inside Yoneko's bones. It was the little priestess, the one they called Thumbelina, and as she spoke she fiddled with a small black box. Later, Yoneko realised that it was a tape recorder which was used for recording any words which were said during her trance so that they could be replayed after it was over. His Reverence would then interpret their meaning as necessary. But now he was instructing them on what was to follow:

'Good evening, ladies. We will shortly establish communication with the spirit world, but first I must warn you about a few dos and don'ts. The world beyond is more terrifying than you can possibly imagine. Every kind of spectral being is to be found there, many of them engaged in endless conflict. However, you are with me, and so long as you do as I say you need entertain no fears. However, should there be any doubting person amongst you, let her be gone! For the presence of such a one can attract the Evil Ones, and draw down upon us their malicious and ferocious power! If such intrude upon our seance, not even I can guarantee that all will go well. But place your faith in me, and nothing untoward will occur!'

He then turned around, and called Miss Yatabe to him. Yoneko observed how, once Miss Yatabe had sat in front of the priest, all the strength seemed to leave her body and throughout the session she seemed to be frozen in terror.

The little medium now proceeded to arrange two

candlesticks, one on either side of Suwa Yatabe. She then nodded to Tomiko Iyoda, who lit the candles and then switched off the electric light in her room. Up until now, it had seemed like a meeting of a discussion group, but with the room in total gloom apart from the two flickering candles, the atmosphere now became eerie.

Yoneko sensed a cold breeze on her neck. She looked around, and was just in time to observe the slight form of Haru Santo slipping in through the door. Haru's hair shone ghostly white in the candlelight as she crept to the cushion beside Yoneko and sat down.

'Link hands with your neighbours!' The priest's voice was full of vibrant power. From Yoneko's left, a clammy hand reached through the darkness and gripped hers. It was Haru Santo who had thus grasped her. Looking to her right, Yoneko could just make out the features of one of the people who had come at the same time as she had, but a sense of revulsion prevented her from reaching out and taking her hand.

'Someone is not cooperating. The seance cannot begin until all hands are linked. Do as I say!'

The priest's voice had become stern and authoritative. Yoneko could not but obey him, unpleasant as it made her feel.

On her left, Haru Santo was chanting the opening lines of a Buddhist Sutra. All around, the others present began to follow suit, until the room reverberated with their nasal tones.

Yoneko began to feel slightly nauseated by the whole proceeding. Someone had lit a bundle of incense sticks, and their powerful scent began to pervade the room.

The priest stood up and spoke.

'Suwa Yatabe, forasmuch as thou hast besought this seance, come now and prostrate thyself before me so that thy spirit shall pass into my keeping.'

He reached down and placed his hands on Suwa's head as he spoke.

She began to mumble disjointedly. From time to time, she seemed to be referring to a violin. At last she fell silent, at which point Thumbelina stood up and began to moan and sway and, eventually, raising her hands on high, to dance in a manner suggesting great exhaustion. In the flickering candlelight, there was something magical about the dance, with two white wrists flickering like butterflies in the gloom. Her long black hair swished from side to side, occasionally falling forward so as to totally obscure her face, then parting slightly to reveal a pale forehead.

Haru Santo began to tremble and shudder, and as she was clasping Yoneko's hand tightly in her clammy grasp, the movement communicated itself to Yoneko's body.

Suddenly, the medium raised her voice to a piercing scream and fell flat on her face. She lay still, but it seemed to Yoneko that she had begun to foam at the mouth, though it might have just been spittle. Her beautiful features, or what could be seen of them through the strands of black hair that lay across her face, seemed to be contorted with pain. Then her tiny body began to shudder and, grinding her teeth the while, she emitted a strange sound.

'Hee, Hee, Hee! Hee, Hee, Hee!'

It sounded like an unpleasant laugh slowed down. Yoneko felt most disturbed. All around her, this strange performance was having the identical effect upon the audience, who sat very still and silent and watched dubiously.

'The seance is now over. Release your hands.' The voice of the priest echoed sonorously in the dark room.

Yoneko took a handkerchief from her pocket and wiped her hands. She felt relieved that it was over, and wished that someone would turn on the electric light, but it looked as if this sect preferred to conduct its business by candlelight. Suddenly she could not bear to stay for a second longer, and she rushed to the lobby and struggled into her shoes, expecting to be halted by a command from the priest, but no one paid her any attention. She opened the door and went out. As soon as she breathed the fresh cold air in the corridor, she felt better.

Within, the sect was continuing its meeting, but Yoneko made her way straight back to her room.

What had she in common with the people in that room, with all their talk of prophecies and revelations and the world of spirits?

She sat down by her desk and reached for the list of her former pupils. But all of a sudden she seemed to have lost the will to continue her series of 'letters from your past'.

Yoneko spent the next two days doing nothing, and hardly daring to leave her room for fear of bumping into Tomiko Iyoda or other members of the Three Spirit Faith. From time to time she overcame her reluctance and went out to have a look at Chikako Ueda's room on the fifth floor. But she had almost given up hope of making any progress in that direction.

On the third day, she was cooking herself a late breakfast when there was a knock on her door. She opened it to find Tomiko Iyoda outside, her face wreathed in smiles.

'What a delicious smell. You're toasting new bread, I suppose!' And without more ado she kicked off her sandals and stepped into the room. Yoneko followed her, apologising as she went.

'I do hope you'll forgive me for leaving so suddenly the other night, after you'd gone to the trouble of asking me. I suddenly felt indisposed.'

There was nothing for it but to offer her unwelcome guest a seat.

'Not at all, not at all. Don't mention it. It quite often happens that way to beginners: the unaccustomed contact with the spirit world overcomes them at first.'

And without the slightest reserve she sat down, looking curiously around the room as she did so, and helped herself to a piece of Yoneko's toast.

'But I felt you'd like to hear the upshot of the seance—it's most interesting, I can assure you. Of course, you realise that funny noise—"Hee Hee"—was a voice from the spirit world? It sounded sad to me, but after you'd gone His Reverence played it back over the tape recorder and explained that in the language of the spirit world that particular sound represents the crackling of flames.

'His Reverence told us that this signified that the missing object had been burned. At which point, Miss Yatabe, the one who'd lost whatever it was—a violin, I suppose—suddenly came out of *her* trance. Well, that should be enough to convince anybody that our seances are genuine, I feel. But there's more and better to come! Would you believe it! Today we had absolute proof of the truth of what His Reverence said. And it happened right before our very eyes—yes, I was there, and saw it, too! Look, I wouldn't have told you this before, but I occasionally had my doubts too, you know. But not any more after this! O how lucky and happy I feel! That's why I rushed straight here to share the good news with you!'

She paused for a sip of tea, and then straightening her fat body she went on:

'Well, you know there's an old brick-built incinerator in the inner courtyard? Yes, well, it'll have to come down because of the moving of the building, so since this morning the labourers have been raking out the ashes and what do you think they found? A violin case! Who could have put such a thing there? Well, it was badly scorched because although it was deep in the ashes, the heat of the fire had reached it. And the poor violin inside was scorched and warped, and the varnish was blistered. There it was, a world-famous instrument of which there are hardly any left, all ruined! Well, Miss Tojo from the front desk said that Miss Yatabe would be the one to know about it, and of course she was dead right, because that was the violin which Miss Yatabe had lost, or rather which had been stolen from her that time when someone broke into her room using the master key, do you remember?

'Poor Miss Yatabe! When she saw the state that violin was in, her knees crumpled and she sat on the floor and cried. For not only was it a famous instrument, but she had received it from her teacher years and years ago. Well, I suppose she shouldn't be blamed, but in her place my first sentiments would be to wonder at the powers of the spirit world and marvel at how His Reverence has penetrated its hermetic secrets! More than the violin itself, his knowing how it would turn out—that's what would move me!

'I mean, that little medium can speak with the tongues of spirits, and of the dead, but there are many who can do that. But His Reverence can understand the language of that world! That is the real miracle if you ask me! It takes the wisdom and experience of someone like him to do that!'

Miss Iyoda seemed to be overcome by her own eloquence. Gradually she calmed down and then took her leave, urging Yoneko to be sure and attend the next seance.

'Now that this has got about, people are coming from all over the building asking if a seance can be held for them. Miss Ueda from the fifth floor is joining us—Miss Santo, one of our most faithful believers, has persuaded her to come. Miss Santo says we all have a positive duty to persuade our neighbours to come, but you know how it is with neighbours—the closer you live to them, the harder it is to make such approaches.'

And she was off to spread the tidings amongst the believers on the third floor.

The news that Chikako Ueda was to attend the next seance gave Yoneko fresh hope. If she had joined the group, then she must be hoping to find out something by means of a seance. So if Yoneko went on attending, then one day Chikako might ask for a seance, and her secret might be revealed. It would take time, but seemed the best and least risky course of action under the circumstances.

Yoneko had thus all but given up her original plan to use the master key to search Chikako's room when, as luck would have it, something happened that very evening to make her change her mind again.

Yoneko had been out to the public bathhouse, and was returning just before the front door was to be locked at eleven pm. Passing into the hall, she suddenly noticed something which she had overlooked before.

Just inside the door was a full set of mail boxes, one for each apartment. On the flap of each there was a tag, marked 'In' on one side and 'Out' on the other, the original purpose having been for residents to change the tag around as they went in or out. Now the paint was faded and on some of them one could no longer read the writing, and so recently people had given up changing the tags when they went out.

Yoneko was looking at the hundred or so boxes and contemplating on how the old practice had died out when she suddenly realised that there was one exception to this rule—Chikako Ueda! Her box read 'Out'.

At that time she imagined it was just an oversight, but the next day she couldn't help looking when she went downstairs, and saw that Chikako's box now read 'In'.

Unless someone was playing practical jokes—and this seemed unlikely—there was only one solution to the problem: Chikako Ueda, who was said never to leave the building, had gone out last night and deliberately changed her tag around!

From this fact, Yoneko could develop two hypotheses. Firstly, Chikako probably took great pains to switch around her tag when she went in or out. This could not just be from force of habit. Yoneko, who had lived a life of solitude for so long, was nonetheless still a good judge of human nature. She reasoned that at first, in the pride of one's new room, one would change the tag every time one entered or left, and that this would go on for a day or so, but would wear thin after a week or so and more or less vanish after two months. And after two years of solitude, who on earth would bother with such a little thing?

And so it wasn't just habit. There had to be a reason, and Yoneko guessed that Chikako was waiting for a visitor.

Her second hypothesis was based on the fact that Chikako only went out just before lock-up time. There had to be a reason for this, too.

She found the answer to this one quite simply. Miss Tamura told her that Chikako would go out once or twice a week to a nearby late-night drapers and obtain her supplies for the embroidery she did in her apartment to keep body and soul together.

'You know, she's so worried about someone calling when she's out that she even leaves her key in the mail box every time she leaves the building! But no one has visited her for years and years. She's an odd one, that's for sure,' confided the receptionist.

When she heard this, Yoneko wished that Miss Tamura had told the story much sooner, although there was no way she could complain about it to her! Perhaps she need never have stolen the master key and undergone the subsequent tribulations. But then, even if Chikako left the key in her mail box, it was right opposite the receptionists' desk, and so it would have been no easy task to remove it and replace it without being seen.

She resolved once again to use the master key to get inside Chikako's room.

As far as the master key was concerned, Yoneko could detect no change in Miss Tojo's attitude towards her since she had switched the keys under her nose, and so presumed that she was not under any suspicion. Also, since the committee had tried the false master key in every door in the building and it had failed to fit even one lock, there was a general presumption that the key had come from outside, and on this vague basis the matter had been allowed to rest. So Yoneko felt that it would now be quite safe for her to use the master key whenever the opportunity presented itself.

She changed her tactics, and no longer went patrolling around Chikako Ueda's room on the fifth floor. Instead, she made it her habit to pass by the front door between half-past ten and eleven every night and check up on Chikako's letter box.

Three days later, her plan worked. She went downstairs to find that Chikako's tag read 'Out'.

She looked out of the front door. There was no sign of Chikako. Around the building, the earth excavated for the move lay in damp brown piles around the conveyors, and the air smelled of freshly turned soil. It was time to make her visit.

She hurried back into the building. The tag on Chikako's box was still moving slightly, so she could not have been gone long. Yoneko hurried to her own room on the fourth floor and collected a torch, a pencil and a notepad. She felt quite calm about what she was going to do. Even if someone saw her going into Chikako's room, she would act as if it was the most natural thing in the world; the last thing she should do would be to look guilty about it. If she behaved like that, then no one would suspect her. She felt quite courageous and resolute as she climbed the staircase.

She passed a woman in a nightdress in the corridor of the fifth floor. The woman was carrying a toothbrush, and disappeared into the communal washplace. Without letting this disturb her, Yoneko went straight to Chikako Ueda's door and inserted the key in the lock. There was nobody around, and Yoneko felt how easy it had turned out to be. She stepped inside the darkened room, closed the door, switched on the torch and looked at her watch. It was ten-forty pm. That gave her ten minutes, during which she must complete her search of Chikako Ueda's room. But what should she concentrate her searches on in that short time?

She swung the torch around the room, focussing the beam on the dusty walls. Obviously the first thing to look for would be a diary. On one side of the room there stood a wardrobe and a chest of drawers. She decided to look inside the drawers.

In the middle of the room there was a low table with a linen towel spread over crockery. It looked like a place setting under the towel, and she lifted it up to find that this was indeed the case, but it was not the kind of setting she had expected in this spinster's room, for the cup was a large one and the chopsticks were of black lacquer and also large. In short, the place was set for a man and not for a woman.

Beside the setting were a few cans of food, a tin opener and a rice tub.

Yoneko felt a cold shiver run down her back. She was inexplicably frightened by this discovery. In order to confirm her suspicions, she opened the rice tub; as she had guessed, it was empty.

When one lives alone, one gets into the habit of talking to oneself. This gives the illusion that one has a companion, and so helps overcome the feeling of solitude. What Yoneko had now discovered seemed to be more or less the same thing. Chikako Ueda, by making a little ritual of setting out dinner for a visitor every night, was fighting her loneliness. But a meaningless ritual would not have this effect—it had to have some basis of fact upon which the fantasy could be built. Some years before, Chikako must have prepared supper for a man who had gone out and never come back. There could be no other rational explanation and Yoneko was convinced that she had discovered something of import.

Next, she tried the smallest drawers in the chest. One was locked and she did not waste precious time trying to open it. The other was full of old receipts and nothing else.

She went towards the window, where there was a writing desk and a bookcase. She let the torch beam play over the book shelves, but from reading the spines of the books it was clear that they were only old school textbooks. There was a pile of notebooks, covered in dust, on the desk, but these were just children's exercise books of the type used for setting homework.

On the other side there was a newer looking exercise book. The word *Elegies* was written on the title page. There then followed two pages of translations from foreign poets; all the works were of sufficient fame for Yoneko to be familiar with them. On the third page, no author's name appeared, but there was a poem entitled 'To a child buried on 29 March'. Yoneko felt that this might prove to be of more interest to her, because of the date and the reference to a child, so she read the whole poem:

TO A CHILD BURIED ON 29 MARCH

We
Buried you
In the bed
Of a dried-up lake
We laid you to rest for ever…

But
The dried bed
Cracked, and sometimes
The sound of your tears
Leaks through and we can hear you…

Why
Did not the merciful heavens
Sprinkle rain at least once upon your dust?
Rain… like the tears of your bereaved mother…

Plainly, the child described in the poem was George, who had been kidnapped from his mother Keiko Kawauchi. Yoneko was certain of this. There was nothing else written in the book. She read the poem once again and tried to learn it by heart, and this time it just seemed like any other poem to her, but she was sure her first impression was right. She wrote down the title in her notepad and got up to go. There was nothing else for her to see.

She switched off the electric torch and closed her eyes. The dull thuds of the work going on outside echoed in her ears—it was time to be gone. She would have plenty of time for thought later.

She turned on the torch again, and looked at the notebook. The beam rested on the title—*Elegies*. She turned to go, and the torch beam, moving with her body, suddenly picked out something bright on the window pane—it was as if a light was being shone inwards at her. She really did not have any more time to spare, but nonetheless she went over to examine this new discovery. It turned out to be the sort of mirror that small boys use to dazzle people in the rays of the sun. What could it all mean?

She slipped out of the room; she heard someone coming up the stairways jabbering away to someone else. She quickly locked Chikako's door and walked briskly to the stairwell. She turned around and looked behind her. She thought she saw a door close quickly further down the corridor; she thought she saw a glimmer of white hair; but she couldn't be sure.

However, it did seem to her rather likely that it was Haru Santo she had seen, and the faint glimpse she had caught of her stayed in her mind for a long time to come.

It was clear from what she had seen that Chikako was still expecting some man to come back to her. But the real possibility of such an event had long since vanished, and only the memory of it now remained, just as fairy tale figures remain in the back of an adult's mind. The preparations for his return had become a daily ritual for Chikako, a reminder of his past presence as real and yet as remote as the sloughed-off skin of a snake one finds by the side of a road. There was no possible interpretation other than absolute fantasy or madness.

Yoneko thought of the white linen cloth and the masculine place setting. What a way to pass one's life! In all her days, despite her occasional hopes, Yoneko had never associated in such a way with a man, and so found it hard to imagine Chikako's feelings.

She wrote to Keiko Kawauchi. Having explained all that had gone on and what she had seen and how she was positive from the size and colouring of the place setting that a man was involved, she went on as follows:

So you see why I am convinced that sometime in the past Miss Chikako Ueda prepared supper for some man who never turned up. I wonder what happened to prevent his coming? Did not this event change her whole life? Since then, she gave up her job as a school teacher and has remained closeted in her room. There is no record of any man having ever visited her.

And so it seems she has waited for six or seven years, laying supper for him every night. Anyone else would surely have given up hope long ago. Why does she refuse to accept the reality of the situation? It can only be because to face facts would be too painful for her. I have heard of other such cases where human beings shut their eyes to the truth in this way.

We have to believe that there was something special about her relationship with this man. We can't be certain, but he may have been involved in George's kidnapping, but if Chikako Ueda was, then it is a fair assumption that he was her accomplice. This bears looking into further.

She put down her pen at this point. The most significant thing she had discovered on her visit to Chikako Ueda's room had been the poem, *To a child buried on 29 March.*

But she still could not bring herself to inform George's mother of this evidence which pointed to the certainty of her child's death. Even if the evidence was even more complete, she cringed at the task. Perhaps it was better for Keiko never to know, for she had based her life on the hope of seeing her child again someday. Could she destroy Keiko's illusions? Even if the man was the kidnapper, had Chikako been directly involved? Certainly she had loved the man, for, even though he had let her down, she had continued to wait for him all these years. Waiting for him had become the purpose of her life, just as it was with Keiko—could she, Yoneko, at one blow destroy the dreams of these two people on evidence which was still only circumstantial? Yoneko began to feel that she had meddled enough in other people's lives already. What had begun as her curiosity about Chikako Ueda's involvement in the kidnapping had reached a stage where Yoneko felt frightened by what she might yet discover.

And so she said no more about what she had found in Chikako's room.

During the next few days, Yoneko could not take her mind off the vision of Chikako Ueda, plying her embroidery needle in her room as she waited for a man who did not come. People lived in a world of fantasy, she reasoned. Chikako Ueda and Keiko Kawauchi shared a similar fantasy. Yoneko felt isolated and empty at the thought that she herself had no such fantasy to give hope and point to her life. This was why her life since retirement had been so blank and meaningless as she felt it was.

Thereafter, Tomiko Iyoda called on her several times to invite her to attend meetings of the Three Spirit Faith, but Yoneko always refused. She did hear that Chikako had joined the group, but she was no longer interested in further spying on her. Perhaps, to the contrary, she was afraid that if she went to the same seance as Chikako she might find out even more about her.

It was not for another few weeks, by which time mid-April had brought clear skies and mild weather, that Yoneko changed her mind and decided to attend a seance.

After getting Yoneko's letter, Keiko had written back urging her to pursue her researches further, particularly regarding the man who had been part of Chikako's life. Yoneko had just put the letters to one side. What made her change her mind about attending a Three Spirit Faith seance was the so-called 'Suwa Yatabe miracle', which occurred during a seance at the end of March. According to Tomiko Iyoda, halfway through her trance, the medium had announced that André Dore, a famous violinist dead for some fifteen years had come in spirit form to announce that he had given his famous Guarnerius violin to Suwa Yatabe. And at this point the priest had opened the charred case to reveal within the Guarnerius restored to its former glory.

'It was indeed a miracle. His Reverence merely touched that burned old violin, and there it was as good as new again! But as if that wasn't enough—yes, there's even more to come—at the same instant Miss Yatabe's finger was mended! You know, she had visited dozens of doctors and none of them could do anything! What powers His Reverence possesses!'

Yoneko, hearing this, was inclined to think that there had been some trickery involved in the miraculous restoration of the violin, but she could not but be impressed by the story of Suwa's finger.

The story spread, so that it was featured in an article in a monthly magazine, and soon hardly a day passed without someone in the apartment block discovering something they had lost, or some prophecy of a relative being involved in a motor accident turning out to be true, all as the result of the Three Spirit Faith seances. And then Tomiko Iyoda told Yoneko that Chikako Ueda was to have a seance to try and locate a missing friend. Yoneko could not repress her curiosity any longer.

'Could I perhaps attend too?'

This time it was she who asked, for Tomiko had let it be known that the growing popularity of the cult had led to capacity audiences and people were having to be turned away of late. However, on this occasion, Tomiko agreed to squeeze Yoneko in as a special concession. The new rule was that to be sure of admittance you had to have attended at least four previous sessions and to make an offering on each occasion of at least one thousand yen.

Yoneko went down to Tomiko's room a full thirty minutes early on this occasion, but there were already some six or seven people in the room when she arrived. The priest and the medium had not yet appeared, and neither had Chikako, on whose behalf the seance was being held. She sat on a cushion in the second row, next to a superior-looking woman in her mid forties who obviously came from outside. Tomiko went around the group and without showing any sign of boredom repeated the same things time and again—how the seances had proved to be of such value, how prophecies had been fulfilled, and how people's lives had been changed thereby and so forth. Her audience were all quite prepared to agree with her, and sat nodding their heads and murmuring assent. It seemed as if this was part of the process of getting people into the right frame of mind for the seance.

At just before eight, the priest appeared, dressed as before in a black double-breasted suit and accompanied by the medium in her red ceremonial priestess' skirt. The audience bowed deeply, sucking in their breath as a sign of respect. There was even one old lady who prostrated herself, touching her forehead to the floor, as the priest passed by.

The priest took his seat, and, addressing a woman in the front row, asked her how her relations with her husband were recently. This made everyone laugh, but Yoneko felt it was a contrived informality and did not join in. This sort of banter and discussion continued for a few more minutes, whereupon the priest broke off and said:

'Leave the door open. The person on whose behalf we are met together tonight is on her way here.'

And the medium lit the candles, as before, and the electric lights were switched off. When the room became thus dark, Chikako Ueda made her entry, accompanied by the white-haired Haru Santo. It was some time since Yoneko had seen Haru, and she tried to catch sight of her face, but somehow there always seemed to be someone else's head in the way. Yoneko reflected that Haru had only come into the room once it was dark on the last occasion, too. Meanwhile, Chikako took up her seat in the very front, facing the medium.

It was the first time that Yoneko had got so close to Chikako. As it was so dark, she could stare at her without embarrassment. In the flickering candlelight, she examined

Chikako's profile and saw a woman who, although in her forties, still had the dimples and fringe of a young girl. There was something very attractively feminine about Chikako, and it looked as if she was a woman who had ceased to age some years back.

As before, the priest adopted a commanding tone of voice and ordered all present to link their hands. Yoneko, thinking that the whole thing was like a staged performance, nonetheless obeyed, although it was with some reservations that she took the hand of the woman from outside who was her neighbour. Chikako then spoke in a clear and firm voice, giving the date of birth and name of the man she sought.

Yoneko tried to work out the age of the man, and found herself confused by the Japanese era system of dates, but at last calculated that he must be in his mid-thirties, and so must have been in his late twenties seven years ago. So he must have been a good ten years younger than Chikako. Could Chikako have had a love affair with a man so much younger than herself? And then Yoneko could not help but think of Keiko, who had married a man more than ten years her senior. In each case, it seemed that the hoped-for bliss had ended in sorrow. Why was it that so many people had such unhappy experiences in love?

While she was thinking over these things, the medium had entered her trance and now once again her whole body was shuddering in the throes of demonic possession.

What happened in the next ten minutes remained engraved in Yoneko's mind for the rest of her life. The medium fell, as before, flat on her face and rolled around on the floor repeating meaningless and garbled words, with an occasional real word mixed amongst them. As these words emerged one by one from the jumbled mass of sound, they stuck in the mind of the hearers, until gradually they could piece together in their minds what was being said. It went like this:

'Ow! It hurts... I can't see anything... I'm in a suitcase, it's hard... A man is putting me into a hole... There's another grown-up with him... A lady! She has opened the bag... She's looking at me... At my face... Now I can hear someone mixing concrete... I see a shovel... Oh, they're shovelling concrete into my suitcase... It's awful... I can't see anything any more... They're burying me in the dark... Mother! Mother!'

This was what Yoneko pieced together, word by word, from amongst the medium's gibberish.

At this point, the priest laid his hands on the medium's head, and cried out, 'Stop! It's the wrong spirit!'

And then, in ringing tones: 'Spirit, I command you to be gone!—Get thee hence!'

Someone in front of Yoneko spoke in a quavering voice.

'Saints protect us! It's an evil spirit in our midst.'

In obedience to the priest's command, the medium became silent and lay motionless, only the whites showing in her open eyes. The priest called for the lights to be put on, and the tension was lowered and everyone stretched themselves in their seats and waited expectantly. The priest called out Chikako Ueda's name.

Chikako did not reply. Yoneko looked at her, and observed that the healthy and youthful appearance she had observed a few minutes earlier had vanished. Now Chikako's whole complexion seemed to have turned grey, and she was staring vacantly into the middle distance, her mouth hanging open, her jaw slack. Tomiko lay her hand on her shoulder and called out.

'Miss Ueda! Miss Ueda!'

Chikako just brushed Tomiko's hand away with an unnatural force. She rolled her eyes up into her lids, and gave every appearance of having entered a catatonic state.

Yoneko left shortly after this, but subsequently heard that Chikako had remained in this condition until the next morning, sitting in the same position staring fixedly ahead. If anyone touched her, she struck the offending hand away.

Haru Santu had slipped out of the room even before Yoneko, and she appeared to have gone at the same time that the lights were turned on.

Making her way back to her room, Yoneko wondered what it was that the medium had said which had had such an effect on Chikako. Could it have been the voice of her lover crying out that he was being buried? Yoneko did not think so. There was clearly some connection between the burial the medium had described and the poem in Chikako's room. This had been the voice of another spirit, and Chikako's reaction and the priest's announcement made the fact doubly clear. The voice had been that of a child being buried, and Yoneko was ninety-nine per cent sure that the child had been George. The medium had been describing the burial of a child in concrete, in terms which rended the heart of Heaven, had used the language of a child describing in terror what was going on before his very eyes.

She realised that she must now tell Keiko Kawauchi the whole truth. She sat down there and then and wrote her a long letter describing in detail all that she had seen and heard, including the poem in Chikako's room. She asked

Keiko to think about it all and apply her own judgment as to what should be done next. She added that it might now be advisable to report the matter to the police.

As she addressed the envelope, Yoneko reflected that she still had some doubts as to whether the dead could really communicate with the living in this way. But there could be no doubting the effect of the words, purporting to come from the dead by way of the medium, upon Chikako Ueda.

It was the last Sunday in April. Yoneko was writing letters in her room when Keiko Kawauchi suddenly appeared at her door. Greeting her after a lapse of some twelve years, Yoneko could not help feeling that Keiko had become rather gaunt, although this may have been the effect of her wearing a Japanese kimono. It was too late to cry over spilt milk, but nonetheless Yoneko wished she had not written to tell Keiko so clearly that George was dead.

Keiko explained that she had been visiting Hiroshima when Yoneko's last letters reached her home.

'As George died at the end of March, it was exactly seven years since his murder. I went to Hiroshima because I heard of a mixed-blooded child of his age there, but of course it was a fruitless trip. And when I got home the day before yesterday, I found your letter waiting for me.'

Keiko wiped the tears from her eyes.

Yoneko did her best to console her, but could do so with little conviction.

There was no positive proof that Chikako Ueda had been involved in the kidnapping. It was by no means certain that the words which had issued from the medium's mouth were George's. What was undoubted fact was Chikako's extraordinary reaction to them. And there was also nothing to suggest that the words did not relate to George. Regardless of whether or not the medium had supernatural powers, or had learned of the facts by other means, it remained obvious that a child had been buried and that Chikako was somehow involved.

And the evidence for this went further than Chikako's behaviour at the seance, for there was also the evidence of the poem Yoneko had found in her room... *To a child buried on 29 March*... it was too much of a mere coincidence.

Of course, there was no year mentioned. It might have referred to 29 March last year, or ten years before for that matter. George had been kidnapped on 27 March, so there was a difference of two days in the dates. But if any evidence could be found that he had been buried on 29 March, then the poem would be conclusive proof of Chikako's complicity.

'If I could be positive that George was dead, then I could at least begin my life all over again.'

Keiko bent low, covering her face with her slim white hands. Looking at her, Yoneko for the first time saw her former pupil revealing her natural maternal instincts.

That night, Keiko stayed in Yoneko's room. They talked until the small hours. Occasionally they spoke about the past, and what had become of Keiko's schoolmates, but for most of the time George was the main topic of discussion. Yoneko felt keenly how Keiko had, for the seven years since the kidnapping, lived only in the hope of seeing her son again, and her heart bled for her. She could not but blame the father who had turned his back on the problem and on his wife and had gone home to America alone, but she could also sense how difficult it must have become to continue living with a wife whose only thoughts were for her vanished child.

'While we were in the waiting room together, George was looking at a comic. When it became his turn to go in, he left it face down on the table, and he was going to finish it later. When he came out from his treatment, he looked for the comic, but a middle-aged American woman was reading it by then. I thought of telling her that my son had been reading it, but felt too shy to do so. Sometimes, when I look back on it, I feel that if he had had that comic to read, he would never have left the waiting room and gone back to the car, and my heart is full of hatred for that white woman.'

Keiko laughed bitterly as she said this, and suddenly Yoneko realised that if she could produce positive and final proof of George's death it would in the end be for the good of her former pupil. Keiko's whole life and personality had become distorted by the uncertainty about her child's fate.

Since the seance, Chikako Ueda had become even more of a recluse, and there seemed no way that anyone could approach her. To get any further in her enquiries, Yoneko realised that she must invent some pretext for talking to Chikako. Even after Keiko went home the next morning, Yoneko spent the day thinking of nothing else.

That evening, when she was just going out to do some shopping, Miss Tojo called out to her from the front office: 'You forgot to register your overnight visitor, you know.' Her face was smiling, but behind the mask Yoneko could detect some suspicion about her relationship with Keiko.

'Perhaps you'd care to fill in the book now?' She pushed the register across the desk, pointing to a clean page.

Yoneko could just discern the traces of writing on the other side.

'I don't want to be petty, but it's always been the rule, you know... We've filled in without fail ever since the war ended, and I suppose we'll go on doing so for another four or five years, even though society has changed.'

And she chatted on in this vein whilst Yoneko registered Keiko's visit. Suddenly, she had a flash of inspiration. Having entered Keiko's name and filled in the relationship column—'friend'—she turned the pages back rapidly until she came to the year 1951. And, just as she had begun to inspect, there was an entry for Chikako Ueda. Ignoring Miss Tojo's astonished and increasingly loud complaints at this breach of the rules, Yoneko gazed triumphantly at the evidence which lay before her, proof positive of Chikako's involvement in the kidnapping.

Chikako Ueda was shown as having had a younger female cousin to stay with her between 29 March and 1 April 1951. The name was given as Yasuyo Aoki, aged thirty, unemployed. As George was kidnapped on 27 March, it seemed clear that this 'female cousin' was the kidnapper who had brought the child to the apartment block.

'Oh, I remember,' Yoneko interrupted Miss Tojo. 'This was the cousin of Miss Ueda's who came with a little boy of about four. He must be getting quite big now.'

Miss Tojo thought for a moment, and then replied, 'No—she was quite alone—I'm sure of that.' She looked Yoneko straight in the eye as she said this, taking the book back and putting it in the drawer. Yoneko felt that one leg of her hypothesis had been knocked from under her.

She went back to her room and retraced every development since she had received Keiko's first letter up to this latest discovery in the guest register. She noted down on a sheet of paper those points which she felt to be of most significance:

1. Chikako Ueda had the opportunity of knowing about George from reading her pupil's essay…
2. She has been awaiting the visit of a man for several years, and always prepares a meal against his coming.
3. She at least knows that a child was buried, and was probably involved in it, too.
    Reasons: (*a*) The poem in her room.
                     (*b*) Her reaction to the medium.
4. During the few days immediately following George's disappearance on 27 March 1951, Chikako Ueda had a female cousin to stay with her.

Having set this all down in black and white, she then examined these facts against the hypothesis that Chikako Ueda was an accomplice in the kidnapping and that the man for whom she had been waiting for so long was the kidnapper. And she suddenly realised that, if this was so, then the young female cousin, the man who had not come back, and the kidnapper were one and the same person. Why had she not stumbled on this obvious fact before? Because she had started off with the false proposition that, because it was strictly forbidden, it was impossible that any male could spend the night in the K Ladies' apartments. And of course not only Yoneko would fall into this trap—it seemed probable that anyone would.

The kidnapper, either under the pressure of necessity or as part of a prearranged plan, had disguised himself as a woman and passed himself off as Chikako's cousin and spent two nights with her. Seen in that light, the K apartment block would be the safest hideout imaginable.

The more she thought about it, the more horrified she became. As each clue fell into place, it became clear what had happened. She pictured the course of events and visualised the young man dressed as a woman standing in front of the reception desk, just where she had herself stood only a few minutes before, sheltering behind Chikako's skirts. Could he have possibly brought George here alive? It would be no easy matter to smuggle in a four-year-old child, to keep him quiet, and so... he had naturally killed him! He had put the body in a rucksack, or suitcase, or some such container, and carried it here. If one was to believe what the medium had said, he had brought him in a suitcase. With what fear of being detected the two of them had climbed the stairs all the way to Chikako's room on the fifth floor! But where had they buried the child? Unquestionably, somewhere in the building. In the inner courtyard? Under the incinerator, perhaps?

At least one thing was clear. There was now no doubt in Yoneko's mind of Chikako's connection with the kidnapping.

Chikako had pledged herself to a man, and waited for him ever since. The man, the kidnapper, had made a promise to Major Kraft, George's father, and had failed to keep it. He had betrayed Chikako and the Major.

She pondered this a while, and then the germ of an idea grew in her mind. Suddenly she saw everything in a blinding flash of inspiration. The man had not betrayed Chikako and the Major—something, some unforeseen accident had prevented him from doing what he said he would. There was no way in which she could deduce precisely what had happened, but she felt that this explanation fitted all the circumstances.

She looked at her clock. It was two am. In the far distance, she heard the baleful whistle of a steam engine. Yes, beyond doubt, the kidnapper was the man Chikako had awaited so long.

All that remained to be discovered was where the child lay buried.

She got into bed and turned out the light. Gazing into the impenetrable darkness of her room, she puzzled over something else. How could the medium have come to know about Chikako's secret? She did not believe in the claims of the supernatural power made by the Three Spirit Faith. For example, if the voice they had heard was truly that of George, it seemed unlikely that he would have used the standard Japanese word for *Mother*. Keiko had said that he addressed her by the English word *'Mummy'*.

This thought frightened her. It meant that, far from the Three Spirit Faith having supernatural capabilities, someone, and that someone closely connected to it, knew of what had happened and was plotting some deep scheme. But who? And why?

At last, her vision blurred in the dark and she fell asleep.

The mist which had begun to settle on the streets an hour before now enveloped the town; nonetheless, it was quite a warm evening and one could just see the naked bulbs, strung around the trench at four-metre intervals to prevent people from falling into the excavation under the apartment block.

The myriad lights of the amusement area below twinkled and died out one by one under the veil of the mist. Yoneko gazed at them in fascination. She was leaning out of the window in the rear corridor on the fifth floor. She had tried every trick she could think of during the last fortnight to get Chikako to let slip where the child was buried but it had all been a waste of time. She had even tried phoning from outside. She had chosen a telephone box in a lonely area and, having called the building, waited for a few minutes while Chikako was summoned from the fifth floor. She had stuffed a handkerchief into her mouth, and, being unused to practising deception, felt thoroughly ashamed of what she was doing. At last she heard the echoes of footsteps approaching the phone at the other end, the sound of the receiver being taken up, and Chikako's breathing. She could visualise the scene at the other end, and felt as if somehow all her efforts to conceal her identity would fail. Disguising her voice and speaking through the handkerchief, she said, 'I know you buried the child. Say where, at once! I know it's in the apartment block.'

She tried to be as threatening as possible. But Chikako said nothing. Instead, Yoneko could hear, first of all, the sound of the phone being dropped, and then the voice of Miss Tojo calling out Chikako's name.

Thereafter, she spent several days racking her brains to think of some other technique. Every day she went into the inner courtyard and looked at the latest diggings. The incinerator and the greenhouse had been removed and the earth all turned over, but there was no sign of any childish bones having been dug up, and no tales of such an event either. She examined the earth and clay which had been dug out from the foundations and dumped by the conveyor on the ground above. Sometimes, she thought she could sense the presence of a rotting corpse, and her stomach turned. Once the soil had been removed, the workmen tamped down the earth under the walls of the building and laid heavy girders and rails. At this point, Yoneko began to doubt if it really was true that a child was buried somewhere in the vicinity. At such times, the words of the medium, the poem in Chikako's room, and all the other pieces of evidence she had so carefully assembled seemed to amount to no more than her wild fancies. But she could not drive out of her mind the conviction that there was a child buried somewhere around the building. The tale of the man who had spent the night in Chikako's room disguised as a woman, and of Chikako who had waited for him all the long years since, now took a second place in her mind. She was possessed by the illusion of the child buried beneath the building and there was nothing she could do about it. Before falling asleep at night, she saw in her mind's eye the site after the building had been moved, with a suitcase somewhere in the centre. But Keiko's son, George, was alive and well and moving around inside the suitcase.

These imaginings were to stand her in good stead when she had all but given up hope of getting Chikako to talk. She made a plan based on them. As soon as the building had been moved, she would rush to Chikako's door, knock loudly, and shout out 'They've found the child's body!'

This should at least produce some reaction which would be of use.

For this plan to work, it would be necessary to prepare Chikako's mind with a few hints of what lay in store for her. So for the past several days she had written 'A divine revelation' on a half sheet of rice paper such as was used by oracles at shrines and pushed it under Chikako's door. The 'divine revelation' that Yoneko wrote read as follows:

'When the building is moved, then all the sinful events that lie buried beneath it shall be revealed. And lo! the child thou didst bury shall come back to life!'

At just about the same time, a rumour went the rounds that a miracle would occur when the building was moved. It was said that the Three Spirit Faith had revealed that a child, kidnapped seven years ago, would be discovered. This gave Yoneko the horrible feeling that someone knew what she was up to! She felt as if all the guilt she was trying to expose was turning around, piling on her. If the Three Spirit Faith made such an announcement, it was clearly part of a human and not a supernatural plan. She felt that this plot would come to fruition before her very eyes on the day that the building was moved. As the instant when the building was to be moved came closer and closer, Yoneko felt more and more like a gambler whose fate rests on one hand, lying face down on the table, which is about to be turned over and exposed. For good, or perhaps for ill…

Only two days remained until the building would be moved. All preparations were complete. The workers had nothing left to do, and peace and quiet had at last returned to the inner garden which lay hidden in the mists below.

Somewhere, she heard a clock strike eleven pm. Yoneko straightened up and made her way towards Chikako's room in order to pass the folded rice paper under her door. As she turned the corner, she heard footsteps on the stairs. Someone was coming. As Yoneko was wearing the patrol armband, there was no need for her to hide or run away. She went to the stairwell and saw Suwa Yatabe coming up to the fifth floor. Suwa bowed slightly as she passed, but her face showed an expression of distaste. She hurried along the corridor and vanished up the stairs which led out onto the roof. She seemed to be carrying an unusually heavy load on her conscience for one who had experienced a miracle, thought Yoneko, and then paused to wonder what Suwa would be doing on the roof at such an hour. However, she stuck to her original plan and made her way to Chikako's room with the 'divine revelation' in her hand. As on all previous occasions, she crept quietly so as not to be heard.

When she got back to the staircase, she thought she could hear a human voice crying out in grief. But it could have been a cat miaowing, or a drunk singing in the road below. All was still again for a moment, and then she heard it quite clearly—the faint sound of a violin being played. It seemed to come from the roof. She heard the vibratos echoing in the night air. She went to the staircase leading to the roof, and as she did so, the sound became louder and then suddenly broke off.

It was pitch dark on the roof. Yoneko stood by the door, creaking on its hinges, and peering into the mist called out: 'Miss Yatabe! Miss Yatabe!'

There was no response. Yoneko took a few steps onto the roof and, raising her voice once again, called out:

'Miss Yatabe!'

The low railing around the roof loomed through the mist, seeming almost to be self-consciously aware of its own existence, but there was no sign of any living being. Somewhere in the distance below, Yoneko heard the shrill squeal of brakes being suddenly applied. She felt suddenly afraid. She froze where she stood, but could hear no sound about her. There was something unpleasant in the air.

The next morning, she awoke to shouts that told her what it was. Suwa Yatabe had committed suicide by jumping from the roof. She had put down the famous violin before leaping to her death, and her body was found on one of the piles of earth which had been excavated from the foundations.

Yoneko reflected on how she and Suwa had passed each other the night before, she on her errand and Suwa hurrying on the way to her death. Now she understood why she had heard the violin but had found no trace of Suwa. Suwa had been bidding farewell to the world on the instrument she loved so much, but Yoneko had interrupted her, and she had gone without completing her tune.

Yoneko felt sad thinking of the last years of Suwa, the violinist whose hopes had turned to sorrow. She did not doubt that Suwa had committed suicide, but one thing puzzled her.

Why, when Suwa passed her on the way to the roof, had she been empty-handed?

On the day of the move, it was windy from dawn on, and dust and grit from the excavations whirled in the air and crept into every corner of the building.

The death of Suwa Yatabe two days before had left everyone stunned, but the excitement of the move now brought things back to life. They got ready for the experiment with the glass of water, which they had looked forward to for so long. Some even made innocent little wagers with cakes or sweets on the outcome. But Yoneko was indifferent to such goings on. She had passed by Chikako Ueda's door once early on in the morning but thereafter had returned to her room to await quietly the hour of noon, and the moving of the building.

She was working out what she should do if her ruse caused Chikako to confess where the child was buried. She had expected to hear from the police after she had revealed all she knew to Keiko, but this had not happened.

She puzzled over where the child could be buried. All the soil around the building and in the courtyard had been dug out to quite a depth, so it couldn't be there. Perhaps under the walls, or the foundations of the incinerator? She remembered the words she had heard about being in a suitcase covered in cement, so such a place seemed likely. Or under the floor? Anyway, if Chikako confessed, she could get the workmen to dig up wherever it was, and then her first action, she decided, would be to call the police.

This led her to imagine Chikako locked up in a cell, which made her feel even worse. She did not enjoy interfering in other people's lives or laying bare their secrets for all to learn. Little had she dreamed, when she began to write to her pupils to overcome the boredom of retirement, that it would end in her exposing someone else and causing her to be dragged off to prison. She began to regret what she had done. Chikako had waited alone in her little room for seven years, and the man had not come; was not this punishment enough? Was it really essential for her to be put at the disposal of merciless public opinion? That would not bring the child back to life.

Yoneko cast her mind back to the three months after her retirement, when she had sat alone in her room gazing at the cold walls. What thoughts had crossed her mind then? Had she reflected back on the life of an old maid who had just let the days go by and life pass with them? She wondered if she had pursued Chikako so relentlessly out of jealously because she had at least had an affair with a man? This thought made her feel she had lost all her strength and purpose.

Reflecting thus upon her solitude, Yoneko glanced down at her watch, which she had put on the table. It was five to twelve. She got up to go to Chikako's room.

Not a soul was to be seen in the corridors or on the staircase, and the whole building was eerily silent.

Just as she reached Chikako's room, the noon siren wailed at a nearby factory. She thought that the building would now begin to move, and rushed to the window but could see nothing to suggest that the move had begun.

She knocked on Chikako's door and turned the knob, but the door was locked. She used the master key to open it. When she got inside, she found Chikako lying with her head on the low table. She had knocked over a glass of water as she fell, and it had dripped onto the floor, where an empty pill bottle had also fallen.

This, then, was Chikako's reply. Was it an admission of guilt or an assertion of innocence? For a second, Yoneko felt dubious, and then she knew the answer. Innocence would not drive one to kill oneself—this was a confession that she had indeed buried the child. She had chosen to die so that the secret would die with her.

Yoneko broke out in a cold sweat, and felt aggrieved at being thus cheated. She dearly wanted to know where the body lay. She looked around to see if there was any sign of a suicide note, but there wasn't. So she would have to work out the answer to the mystery by herself.

At least she now knew for certain that the child was buried somewhere near at hand. Any lingering doubts were overcome by the fact of Chikako's death. So the poem told the truth.

The poem was true... Yoneko grasped the point in an instant.

'The bath! The bathroom! That's it!' Yoneko felt herself shouting inside her heart. The dried-up lake plainly referred to the disused bath in the basement. And seven years ago the cement left over from the repair work interrupted by the war was still lying around that bathroom. Thereafter, it had been removed, and the bathroom used as a storage place for furniture from the communal rooms, old stoves, and so forth.

She rushed out of Chikako's room and down the stairs to the basement. She was determined to break open the bath herself. At that moment, she was no longer the retired old maid but the gambler turning the card which would seal her fate. Life and youth flowed back into her.

Chikako's door was left open, so that anyone passing by could see her lying face down on the table, the spilt water about her.

And the master key remained in the lock, just as Yoneko had left it.

PART EIGHT

Some months after the building was moved

Miss Tojo's Chronicle

I suppose I decided to set this all down in some proper form, as an archive for the future, during those thirty irritating minutes while the move of the building was delayed.

During that half hour, I just gazed at the glass of water which was on the dusty table in front of me, not knowing whether to laugh or to cry. My feelings were not directed at anything or anyone in particular, but at the caprices of fate which can bring about changes in the best laid plans of mice and men, as the saying goes. Fate! It can stab you in the back any time, upsetting the most carefully thought out activities. Fate doesn't care what the upshot is.

I can't put up with such treatment. I feel as if the pride and spirit of the human race is being trampled on. However amusing the upshot might be, it's worth remembering that some human is seeing his important plans crumble before his very eyes.

Well, this present case has been so thoroughly reported in the press, on the radio and in the periodicals that I daresay everyone knows all the details backwards.

Briefly, it was like this. A retired woman with time on her hands was living in the K Apartments for Ladies, a place with some history behind it. Having nothing better to do, she took to writing to all her former pupils, and found that one of them had married a foreigner and had her child kidnapped seven years back and never seen again. And this old teacher suddenly rushes out, at the very moment the building is to be moved, shouting out that the body is buried under the bath. And so they dig up the bath in the basement, and what do they find but a body of a child, just as she said! But, and here's what caused all the excitement, *it wasn't the body of the kidnapped child at all*! It turned out to be the child of a resident of the apartments. He was born deformed so she couldn't bear to bring him up and killed him and buried him!

The mother committed suicide; the old teacher who discovered all this was held by the police for enquiries because she had made unlawful use of the master key; and the celebrated priest and founder of a new mystic religion who had prophesied about the buried child was exposed as a fraud. So you can imagine what a field day the papers and so forth had!

There's no longer any doubt in my mind that the press, in spreading news, takes no account of the bare facts but rather prefers to call everything in question by means of irresponsible reporting. Maybe the gossip of housewives at the laundry, or of strap-hangers in the trams, is true as far as it goes but it doesn't go beyond the surface or get at the real truth behind the facts.

Nonetheless, there was a lot of coincidence involved— what I referred to as 'tricks of fate' earlier. In setting forth this record for future readers, I want to go beyond the different coincidences and their final result. I want to look at what various human beings planned, and what came about as a result.

What follows is in its own way a tiny saga.

The tale begins thirty years ago. A young girl, raised on a farm in Hyogo prefecture, went to Kobe at the age of eighteen and worked as a housemaid in the home of a Christian missionary. By an irony of fate, at the age of twenty-five, instead of marrying a young man, she settled down as receptionist-manageress of an apartment block full of young women. Day in and day out she sat at the front desk, dreaming her dreams, and determined to better herself. She would watch the young ladies of her own age going out to their work, and she would secretly read and read—several books a day, sometimes, keeping them hidden on her knee under the desk. Well, the whole of human life is contained in books. Love, desire, success and failure, death and grief… they're all there, in the world of books.

So she went on sitting at that desk, and her straight little back gradually began to bend a bit, but still she went on reading books and fed and nourished her mind in that way. And one day, before she had time to notice what had happened, she woke up to find that she was forty years old. Suddenly, the shadow of tragedy passed over her at that moment—she didn't know why it was so, but she felt it, and that's what matters.

Apart from her, there was one other receptionist, who was over the regulated age for the job. Just at that very time, the old receptionist suddenly died. The heroine of our story, if we can call her that, was left to clear up the old woman's room and discovered something she had never suspected. You see, there was only supposed to be *one* master key, but the receptionist who died had a spare. It then became clear to the younger receptionist that her senior had used it to steal into the residents' apartments and snoop around. It had become her secret pleasure to spy on the residents when they were out. And, after a year or so, our heroine became addicted to the same perverse pleasure. But she was cleverer and more cautious than her predecessor, and one day, when she slipped on the staircase and twisted her ankle, she feigned lameness even when her foot was better and thereafter went everywhere on crutches. So everyone thought she really was lame.

One more thing contributed to the success of her activities. The new receptionist who joined after the old one died was an amiable body who had the habit of catnapping.

Well, our heroine had one other trick up her sleeve to ensure that she could wander around the apartments at will without attracting too much attention. This was to take on a dual identity and become a resident, at least to outward appearances. During the years she had worked there, at least half the residents had changed. So she chose a vacant room next door to people who didn't talk too much to strangers, and created for herself a second personality. It was quite easy to do, when you think of it, because all the necessary procedures for creating this new identity lay within her purview as receptionist. The apartment was confiscated during the war as enemy property; afterwards, it became a charitable trust and the rents were pegged at wartime levels so our receptionist found it quite easy to maintain her double life.

Well, over a period of years, she got to know the secrets of every room, and thus of every resident. Within their thick walls, and behind their strong doors, what a sedimentation of life those rooms contained! Most people would have broken under the weight of such knowledge, but our heroine was versed in the ways of life from her reading and so she could withstand the pressures of her secret knowledge.

One night, she was in the basement when she saw two women burying a heavy brown leather case in the bottom of the broken tiled bath. They were a resident of the fifth floor and a girl entered in the visitors' register as her younger cousin. Just at that time, the kidnapping of a mixed-blood child became a major topic in the press. Our sagacious heroine was quick to link all these facts and draw her own conclusions. But she kept it all a secret—without realising in what good stead this would stand her seven years later.

Well, she had a younger brother whom she hadn't seen for years. One day, he suddenly appeared, and announced that he was going to found a new religious order together with the Thumbelina vestal. He said he'd studied spiritualism in America, but our heroine didn't believe him for one moment. He was the type who always made a botch of whatever he did. He'd had great ambitions as a boy, but everything had somehow gone wrong. She felt for him the love one can only feel for a close blood relative.

She thought how she could make use of all the secrets she had discovered whilst living her double life, by passing them on to her brother. It may well have been the temptation of the devil.

By now, I am sure that the reader understands that I am that receptionist, the 'heroine' of our story as I called her above.

The breaches of the trust inherent in my job, the immoral actions, or, let's not beat about the bush, the crimes which followed should be seen against the background of my sisterly love. You readers who have grown up in happy homes will not be able to understand the feelings of someone like me who, after living alone for so long, suddenly encounters a chance of escape from this solitude. You will not therefore understand that in such circumstances one is prepared to give up everything rather than lose that chance. All I wanted to do was something, or rather anything, which would help my brother.

I do not believe in the supernatural or in any Divine Being. So when I decided that a few fake miracles would be the best form of publicity for my brother's religious business, I had no feelings of guilt on the matter.

I also felt that I could kill two birds with one stone. The best way to bring about the discovery of the child buried under the bath would be by way of 'miraculous' prophecy from the Three Spirit Faith.

So the trick I played on my colleague Miss Tamura—the phone call which led her to investigate Toyoko Munekata's apartment and discover the meaninglessness of her scholarship—was, like the 'miracle' of Miss Yatabe's violin, just a means to an end. My real objectives were to reveal the buried child and to do so by way of my brother's prophecies.

I realised that it would look suspicious if the Three Spirit Faith were to make a prophecy and then soon discover where the child was buried. It would be much better to use the prophecy to attract some other person's interest so that that other person could be led to discover the body for herself. That way, nobody would doubt the genuine nature of the prophecy.

And, because I knew the secrets of everyone in the building, it should be a simple matter to select the right person for my purpose and lead her, without her knowing, to the discovery I wanted her to make at the right time.

As far as Miss Tamura was concerned, all I had to do was to get my brother to call from outside and drop the hint about Miss Munekata's secret. Being of a good-natured disposition, Miss Tamura would hate having to conceal the phone call, and yet would be equally unwilling to reveal its content until she was sure of the matter for herself. It would then only be a matter of time, I reasoned, before she would use the master key to get into Toyoko's room. Where she slipped up, and my calculations went wrong, was that she left the master key in the lock of Noriko Ishiyama's room instead of returning it to the office. (She thought I was out at the public bathhouse, but in fact I returned early and observed her coming out of Toyoko Munekata's room.)

As my intention had been to spread a feeling of uncertainty around by having her use the master key to go into people's apartments, her mistake in fact served my purpose. But the pains I had to take to get Noriko Ishiyama to use the key were more than you can imagine. I had to devise a way of getting the old newspaper, which I had originally come across in the deceased receptionist's room, describing the theft of the violin into Miss Ishiyama's hands. Then I had to invent a foreigner who came enquiring for a copy of the paper. It was all but impossible, but my plan worked. Then I was lucky enough to spot Noriko Ishiyama hiding the stolen violin in the incinerator, and so could recover it.

(Needless to say, I substituted for it an instrument I bought in a junk shop, which I put into the real case.) This meant that I could bring about the 'miracle' of Suwa Yatabe's violin, but in the end this led to the tragedy of her death, which I much regret.

I must confess that when Miss Yatabe's finger straightened out after the medium had told her that André Dore formally bequeathed the violin to her, I began to believe in miracles myself. However, when my brother, in order to gain more publicity for the 'miracle', went too far and told her to turn herself over to the police and to return the violin to André Dore's son, her face changed colour suddenly and she screamed: 'He had no son. It was you and your fellow conspirators who wrote that fake letter from a foreigner to me.'

Well, that led to us having to push her off the rooftop. By 'us' I refer to the medium and Haru Santo. Of course, as you must by now have realised, Haru Santo was me in my other guise. As I wanted to keep an eye on Chikako Ueda, I waited till the room next to her fell vacant, and then Haru Santo moved in. I registered her name and made out the rental agreement in my official capacity.

So for five years, wearing a white wig, I lived part of every day in the role of Haru Santo. Every evening I would peep in through Chikako Ueda's window. I rigged up a wing mirror from a car on a stick so that I could see what was going on. Every night, she would open the little drawer she always kept locked, take out a cardboard box and gaze at its contents for hours on end. I took it for granted that this was the three hundred thousand yen ransom for George—well, for once I was made to look a perfect fool!

For it turned out that the box contained a certificate of marriage registration, duly sealed, which would acquire the full force of law merely by being delivered to the ward office. I just can't imagine how anyone could spend her evenings for seven years looking at a marriage certificate left behind by some man who had abandoned her, but that's what women are like, I suppose.

Well, in the same way the little medium Thumbelina loves my brother, and it was out of love for him that she was my accomplice in the murder of Suwa Yatabe. She was not actually present, but she lured Suwa to her death by telling her to come to the rooftop at eleven pm and promising to return the violin to her. Suwa, thinking that it was only little Thumbelina she had to contend with, lowered her guard enough for me to push her over the edge.

I had made allowances for someone seeing Suwa going onto the roof and following her there, as indeed Yoneko Kimura did. First of all, I had taken a thick bamboo pole (one of the ones used for drying laundry) and lashed it to the railings so that it led down to Haru Santo's windowsill. I was thus able to make good my escape, and later on I replaced the pole where I had found it. Also, in order to cover Suwa's screams as she fell, I had brought with me a tape of her playing the violin, and played it at the right moment.

All well and good as far as it went, but I never intended to become a murderess. I detest such things, and getting into the position where I had to kill Suwa Yatabe was my big mistake—in the case of Toyoko Munekata, I had no intention of killing her, and indeed she survived the gassing. I just wanted to punish her for her overwhelming pride, and saw my opportunity when she descended on me the day before, berating me in her usual haughty manner because her fanlight window wouldn't shut. So I knew perfectly well that if I turned off the gas from outside and then turned it on again, I could teach her a good lesson but without fatal consequences.

I pretended not to notice when Yoneko Kimura switched the master key, and I think my plans there went off very well. You see, Miss Kimura stood apart from all the others, being much more intelligent than the average and also possessed of abundant common sense. A person just like me, in fact, and so it was very easy for me to foresee how she would react to any given occurrence and make my dispositions accordingly. So I made sure that by one means or another she got to know everything that I knew about Chikako Ueda. For instance, I had witnessed the burial in the bathroom, but could by no means impart that directly, so instead I just wrote that elegy and left it in Chikako Ueda's room for Yoneko to read. Then I made sure she would hear the right things from the medium, and that she would get the chance to see the register of overnight visitors... I led her, by these three clues and by other means, along a process of deductions which culminated in the understanding I wished her to have. I felt just as if I was the director, and got great pleasure out of seeing my actress perform her role exactly as I wished.

But my masterpiece as far as she was concerned (and I'm sorry to keep harping on my own brilliance, but that, after all, is the theme of this document)—the high point of my direction—was young Kurokawa. You remember, of course? He was the former playmate of George's who wrote an essay titled 'My little foreign friend' for his teacher, Chikako Ueda. Yes, well, that was my doing, too.

It was like this. After witnessing the burial in the bathroom, I passed many a day seated at my desk wondering what was the connection between Chikako Ueda and George. I worked out all sorts of possible theories, but they were all too far-fetched for me to believe in with any conviction. So I bought and read everything that had been published about the kidnapping—quite a pile of newspapers and magazines, but standing, as it were, on top of that pile I could see over the wall and discover the connection. And what caught my eye was a remark made by the maid in Major Kraft's household. 'My son was very close to George, and they used to play together.' It was like playing three-cushion billiards; there was no direct link between Chikako and George, so I had to make an indirect connection. I worked on the supposition that the maid's child had been a pupil of Chikako's. If that were the case, then it might well have been that he mentioned George to his school teacher. Or, to carry it further, he might have written an essay about his little foreign friend. And that essay could have planted the dreadful idea of the kidnapping in Chikako's mind. This sort of set of circumstances would at least provide a firm linkage between Chikako and George.

But I did not even have to ascertain whether this was true or not. After all, I was by then using Miss Kimura to carry out the investigation without her knowing that I was manipulating her behind the scenes. It would be quite enough to plant in her mind the idea that such an essay might have been written.

My brother, the little vestal and I went to great pains to ensure that everything was adequately prepared for the great prophecy which would reveal the child's tomb. For example, we timed the revelations one by one against the schedule of works for the moving of the building. In this case, we hired a detective agency to report on Keiko Kawauchi. My brother carried out this part of the plan very well. When we learned that Keiko used to visit the neighbourhood of her old home in Denenchofu every day, I decided to pull young Kurokawa out of my conjuror's hat.

I timed that, too. I kept a close eye on Yoneko Kimura's progress through the register of her former pupils, and it was only when I knew that she was about to write to Keiko that I produced young Kurokawa. My brother, by dint of his persuasive tongue plus a thousand-yen note, was able to hire a student of the right age to perform the role. He did it quite well enough to convince Keiko that such an essay had been written.

As I used this device to draw together Keiko and Yoneko Kimura, who had been as it were 'in another part of the forest', I felt just like a theatrical director using the revolving stage to bring his characters together. And the roots, deep as they were, of these plans went back beyond the reappearance of my brother, right back, indeed, to the time George had been kidnapped. They went back seven years to the time when Yoneko Kimura had stood in the porch reading the evening paper, and looked up and told me 'The mother of this child who has been kidnapped was a former pupil of mine'. I paid no particular heed at the time, but looking back, it must have been that my subconscious mind was already linking and drawing together Keiko Kawauchi, Yoneko Kimura and Chikako Ueda.

So many years spent in a gloomy office, thinking and plotting, and to what avail? Fate made a fool of me in the end, after all.

Yoneko and I were both made the puppets of mocking fate. You see, when Yoneko rushed down to the bathroom, she got the workmen to dig up the bath, and indeed there was a child buried there, so they called the police.

But after the autopsy, it became hideously clear that we had been deceived. When I think of it, I still beat my head in disgust. Can anyone disagree with me when I say that both Yoneko and I were like children building magnificent sandcastles only to see them washed away by the tides of fate? Why did my three positive facts turn out to be the foundations for a sandcastle?

The papers and magazines have speculated quite enough on how it came about that Chikako Ueda had given birth to a child, and what abnormality it was which caused her to kill it. I will not touch any further upon the matter, particularly as it is distasteful to me. It drains the blood from my veins even to consider that the child I saw being buried was Chikako's own son.

All I want to know is, whatever happened to the child who was kidnapped? I'm prepared to lose everything which remains to me in return for knowing that. After all, what is left to me? My brother has gone. Haru Santo can no longer peep into Chikako Ueda's room, for she is no more. Life is just a passing dream, and we are the toys of mocking fate.

Perhaps, after all, there is a God who watches over our doings and who has punished me by changing the body I saw buried for another body. Well, I'd feel happier if I could think it was so. At least, it would give me some comfort to think that I was the victim of a sentient being and not of blind fate.

But my destiny is now clear. I must pass the remaining years of my life, seated at this lonely desk with no one to talk to. All I can do is write this record and then puzzle, and puzzle… all to no avail.

I rack my brains trying to work out what became of the kidnapped child, even though I realise there is no way of knowing.

That way lies madness.

EPILOGUE

In a pleasant suburb of Los Angeles, Major D. Kraft (US Army, Retired) lay back in a deckchair on the lawn of his garden. He puffed at a pipe as he scanned the newspaper, and then he saw, tucked away in the corner of an obscure page of foreign news, a small item concerning Japan.

He looked up at the sky, and fixed his attention on a small cloud. He was remembering a certain Japanese girl. Whenever he thought of her, his conscience was disturbed.

'Well, I suppose worse things went on during the Occupation,' he mused. 'What the hell else could I do? I mean, my wife and I had lived apart so long... and then she suddenly arrives in Japan, and we start up all over. Besides, she was rich, and I had to think about my retirement. A major doesn't get much of a pension, and anyway I didn't want to stay in the army for ever. I needed a bit of security for a change.

'In return, my wife just wanted me to get rid of my Japanese girl, but to bring the child I had had by her over here so we could bring him up as our own. Well, in fact I'd gone through a proper marriage with the Japanese girl, and I didn't want to be up for bigamy, so it was pretty scary.

'After I had collected George from the car, I took him straight to the airport and put him on the next plane Stateside. My wife had quite a job calming him down, but that was her problem.

'Well, I went back to my Japanese home, and I guess I really meant to tell my Japanese wife the truth. But, hell, when I saw her face, I just couldn't bring myself to do it.

So I just said, "Don't worry, honey, I'll call the police," and I was just leaving when the phone rang.

'Well, I answered it, and it was just one of my buddies inviting me round for a game of poker. My Japanese dame was looking at me, kind of worried-like, and that gave me the idea of the kidnap story. So I just said "OK" and put the phone down and told her that it was the kidnappers, and that if we called the police there was no way we'd get to see George again.

'Well, then I nearly blew it. I mean, that kid trusted me so much, I got over-confident and ran those ads in the Japanese press, and then some pressman got hold of them and the shit hit the fan. So I had to keep up the story about how if I talked to the police or the press, the kidnappers said I'd never see George again.

'I then just waited for time to pass, and when things quietened down, I divorced that Japanese wife and went back to the American one.'

He puffed at his pipe.

Just then a little girl ran along the pavement across the road. She was in tears.

'George is teasing me again!'

Major Kraft looked up, and saw George's school teacher leading his son towards him by the scruff of his neck.

━━━

AVAILABLE AND COMING SOON
FROM PUSHKIN VERTIGO

Jonathan Ames

You Were Never Really Here

Augusto De Angelis

The Murdered Banker
The Mystery of the Three Orchids
The Hotel of the Three Roses

María Angélica Bosco

Death Going Down

Piero Chiara

The Disappearance of Signora Giulia

Frédéric Dard

Bird in a Cage
The Wicked Go to Hell
Crush
The Executioner Weeps
The King of Fools
The Gravediggers' Bread

Friedrich Dürrenmatt

The Pledge
The Execution of Justice
Suspicion
The Judge and His Hangman

Martin Holmén

Clinch
Down for the Count

Alexander Lernet-Holenia

I Was Jack Mortimer

Boileau-Narcejac

Vertigo
She Who Was No More

Leo Perutz

Master of the Day of Judgment
Little Apple
St Peter's Snow

Soji Shimada

The Tokyo Zodiac Murders
Murder in the Crooked Mansion

Masako Togawa

The Master Key
The Lady Killer

Emma Viskic

Resurrection Bay

Seishi Yokomizo

The Inugami Clan